Crashing Into You

Copyright

Disclaimer

The books in this series are based completely on dreams that I've had or that one of the other people in my relationship has had. They all have a little bit of real life thrown in so that you, the reader, can get to know us a little bit better.

These books can and should be read as standalone books. There isn't an order to them. All of the characters in the books are the same, as they are all based on characters from real life.

As you read these books, please keep in mind that other than the characters and the city they are based in, these books are not connected to other books in the series. They aren't a continuation of other books. They are all novellas based on dreams that revolve around the same characters.

As you keep that in mind, please enjoy reading this book. I do hope you will also read the others in this series and love them as much as I loved writing them!

Opening Quote

Your lips are on my lips, and our hearts beat as one, but you slip out of my fingertips every time you run. Don't wanna break your heart. Wanna give your heart a break. I know you're scared it's wrong. Like you might make a mistake. There's just one life to live. And there's no time to wait. So let me give your heart a break. Let me give your heart. 'Cause you've been hurt before. I can see it in your eyes. You try to smile away some things you can't disguise. Don't wanna break your heart. Baby, I can ease the ache. So, let me give your heart a break.

Give Your Heart A Break by Demi Lovato

Chapter One

☆ Lyric ☆

I grip his wrists and claw at his hands. The air I need is being cut off. He squeezes my neck harder.

I fight.

Thrash.

The edges of my vision slowly start to darken. I'm going to lose consciousness soon.

I scratch him.

My lungs burn.

My head is fuzzy.

My throat aches. I feel like my trachea is going to collapse at any moment.

I try to scream, but no sound comes out. The room is getting darker and darker. I'm getting weaker and weaker. My grip on him starts to slacken more and more. I'm not going to make it through this time.

"Lyric!" a deep male voice yells.

I flinch, even though it's so far away. Like he's screaming at me from a great distance.

"Lyric!" The voice is closer now.

I can feel a hand on my arm. It's pulling me.

"Lyric! Wake up!"

He's shaking me. But who? I know the voice.

"Lyric! Come on. Wake up!"

My eyes snap open. My hands fly to my throat as I gulp in lungfuls of air.

It's dark.

Goosebumps erupt on my skin. Every single part of me is stiff and cold.

Wet.

I'm soaking wet. My hair. I run my fingers through it. Soaked. My body feels drenched. I'm shivering uncontrollably. I take breath after breath. My lungs are on fire. A stark contrast to the ice prickling my skin.

I blink as I try to figure out where I am.

Where *he* is.

Where are his hands? They were around my neck. He was squeezing the last bit of life out of me. He was finally getting his ultimate wish.

I sniffle and take another breath. My chest still feels like it's collapsing. My throat is hoarse. I close my eyes a moment before opening them again. I take another breath, slowly coming back to myself.

I look down at the hands on my arms, then up. "Luca," I say, relieved.

He smiles, but doesn't release me. "Yes. Luca. Are you coming back to me?"

I let out a breath and nod. "Yes. I… I'm sorry."

"Don't be sorry. I know better than anyone what you went through." He kisses my forehead before getting up slowly and walking to my bathroom. I hear the water running moments later.

I take a second to look around the room. I jump when I realize I'm naked and groan. "Gross." I take the blanket and pull it over my head when I lay down.

"Nope. Up." Luca grabs the blanket and tries to pull it back.

I grip it tighter. "Go away."

"Not a chance. Your shower is ready, princess." He tries to yank it down again and succeeds because he's stronger.

I cover my chest, but the effort is pointless. Luca has his head turned and is holding up a towel for me. "Oh." I take the towel and wrap it around myself as I get up. "Thank you."

"Seeing my sister naked wasn't exactly how I planned to wake up. But you were screaming, so I set it aside."

I sigh. "I thought I was doing better."

"Well, you are. But we've discussed this. It takes time to get over what happened to you. You went through a lot, Lyric."

I sigh and reach up to wipe a tear away. "I need to take a shower." I try to give him a strong and brave smile, but I've never been able to hide anything from him. I know he sees right through me.

Luca watches me as I make my way to the bathroom. I take a breath and turn to close the door, but I stop. I look up at my brother and bite my lip, suddenly feeling shaky and more than a little afraid.

"You don't need to close the door," he says softly. "I'm right here. Just like I always have been."

I give him a grateful smile as I step behind the door and hang my towel on the hook before stepping in the shower. I let the warm water cascade down my body, washing the sweat from the dream away.

I let out a breath and wrap my arms around myself. The dreams aren't unusual, but they are few and far between. Ever since I moved to the United States from my homeland in the United Kingdom, they've become less frequent. I credit the distance between me and everything the United Kingdom holds.

Ever since I was a child, I'd dreamed of visiting the United States. But the older I got, the more I wanted to just move. I wanted to live here. I love everything about the United States. I love American football and American food. I love all of the pastimes and music.

I love that, in America, there are more freedoms. A person can be themselves, for the most part, without being looked down on. In the United Kingdom, a person has to behave a certain way. If they don't, it's like they are shunned.

I love reading about places that have ranches. I fell in love with the small towns that truly have a small-town feel. I love American TV shows. They seem to portray a close-knit family bond. Something I never had.

Besides my twin brother. We're fraternal twins. I feel like Luca managed to get all the looks and height and good characteristics that everyone loves. Luca was always popular in school. He never had to work to make friends. He excelled at everything he attempted. He never had to try at sports or studying. Everything came naturally to him.

My parents always doted over him. My entire family did. Luca was the perfect child to them. If he ever did anything wrong, they overlooked it. If I did, I was punished. I would get screamed and yelled at. I was often sent to my room and expected to sit there and be a good girl. I wasn't expected to talk. I was expected to study.

I'd always been quiet. And for some reason, that was an invitation for kids in high school to pick on me. What started as teasing, though, turned into something a lot more vicious. I was never a model size zero. I wasn't fat, but I had curves. I didn't like wearing clothes that showed off my assets. I didn't fit in with the other kids when it came to fashion. I was a wallflower. An outcast.

I shiver when the water turns cold and shut it off. Apparently, I've been in here a lot longer than I thought. That happens a lot, too. I get lost in thought and lose total track of time. What feels like a few minutes to me could be hours in reality.

I grab my towel and wrap it around me, then take another to dry out my hair. I step out of the shower, breathing deeply. I always feel out of sorts after a dream like that. I've worked so hard to move on. But sometimes, I get pulled back. I don't like not being able to control it.

I walk out to my room and notice Luca has made the bed. My sheets are in the clothes basket. Luca is straightening the rest of my room. I watch him for a moment and smile softly at how lucky I am to have a brother like him.

Luca has always been my hero. When the bullying started, Luca always did all he could to stop it. He couldn't be with me all of the time, but he tried to be. He didn't like hearing about someone tripping me or slamming me into a locker. He hated it when he came across me laying on the floor after being pushed. Luca has never been able to stand seeing me cry. It took all of his willpower while we were in school to not end up suspended or expelled for fighting.

The older we got, the more protective Luca became. I think that probably happened because he didn't feel like he did enough for me in school. I was hit and kicked. I was shoved. He didn't like that he couldn't protect me from all of that. So, as we aged, we became closer, and Luca became more defensive of me.

"I changed your sheets," Luca says quietly.

I shake my head to rid myself of the thoughts and look up at him. I don't know when he stopped tidying things and came to stand in front of me. I give him a soft smile. "Thank you."

He gently puts both hands on my face and tilts my head from side to side as he studies me. After a few moments, he kisses my forehead and lets me go. "I'm supposed to have lunch with DJ. Are you going to be okay? I'll cancel."

I shake my head. "I need to go into work. We have the Police Officer's Grand Ball. I need to make sure everything goes off without a hitch. I also have a birthday party this weekend that I need to work on. I only have two days to make sure everything is finalized. Besides, DJ is your only friend here." I lower my eyes.

Luca doesn't do well without friends. He's always been social. He thrives on it. I've never met this DJ person, but whoever he is, Luca has taken a liking to him. I'm grateful to him. Luca uprooted his entire life to move here with me.

"Hey, Lyric. Don't. I have no regrets. I would have left in a heartbeat if it meant protecting you." He hugs me tightly. I let myself relax in his arms and soak in his strength. "How about you get dressed, and I'll drive you to the Thomas Center on my way to meet DJ?"

I smile softly and nod. "I'd like that. I'm not really in the mood to drive or take a Lyft."

He slowly lets me go. "Good. Then it's settled. I'll make something light for you to take with. It's nearly eleven. We'll need to leave soon."

I nod again. "I'll be ready." I smile bravely, slowly gaining back the strength the dream took from me. He smiles and kisses my forehead again. He makes his way out of the room. "Luca?"

He turns back to me. "Yeah?"

"Thank you. For helping me all the time and never making me feel stupid or weak."

"Lyric, you're not stupid. You're sure as fuck not weak." He watches me for a moment. "Get dressed."

I do what I'm told with a soft smile. Luca has never understood it, but he really is like a superhero to me. He may be my twin brother, but to me, he's more than that. We've never had a rivalry like most siblings. Even when our parents tried to pit us against each other somehow. When I got disciplined for something that they knew he did, Luca always tried to stick up for me. He'd even talk to me in my room afterwards. I'm sure it pissed our parents off.

We're very different, though. It never ceases to amaze me how we managed to stay so close despite how truly different we are. Our looks are similar, but different. Where Luca is six feet, I'm only five feet three or four. Where Luca has muscle, I have soft features. I don't have much muscle tone. Compared to him, I'd be considered a mouse next to a lion.

We share the same dark hair and golden hazel eyes, but even our skin tone differs. Luca has acclimated quite well to the climate change we live in here in Gainesville, Florida. He has managed to tan well. My skin is fair. While I do end up tanning, I first burn. It doesn't seem to matter how long I'm in the sun or how dark my skin ends up. If I'm not wearing sunscreen, I become a lobster before I gain that drool-worthy, sun-kissed look that comes so effortlessly to Luca.

I check my reflection in the mirror when I finish getting ready and smile softly as I start fixing my hair. I have put on a few pounds that I am proud of since moving here. After the bullying started, I began dropping weight. The stress was pretty bad.

But it was the relationship that came afterwards that really caused a problem. I lost a lot of weight. I barely survived. If Luca hadn't helped get me out, I probably wouldn't have.

But after…

I take a breath, refusing to go there. We moved to the United States just over a year ago. We both got jobs rather quickly. I love mine. I know Luca loves his. He's always loved to work with his hands and build things. He's worked in construction for as long as I can remember. It wasn't hard for him to get a job here. There's always a need for construction workers. Luca loves helping people. Seeing a building or house finished fills his heart with warmth.

It's much like me. I managed to get a job when we got here as an event planner. I had done several small birthday parties. I was even able to have a hand in a few small events. When the Historic Thomas Center put out an ad for a position as an event planner, I jumped at the chance. I knew the position would be hard to get. Lots of people applied.

It was my application, though, that caught the director's attention. I still don't fully understand how. There were lots of people who applied who had tons of experience with weddings and huge charity galas. During my interview, though, I was told that my unique decorations and ability to make small parties on a small budget seem like giant events with no regard for spending at all was truly astonishing.

I wasn't guaranteed the job right then, but I ended up getting it. Since then, I've been planning and decorating for different types of events. I love what I do just as much as Luca. Seeing the faces of my clients light up is such a highlight for me. I don't need praise or compliments. Just seeing how happy they are when they walk in and see the venue is everything to me.

I walk out to the room and take the strawberry banana shake Luca made for me. "Ready to head out?"

He smiles. "Yeah. When you are."

"I'm ready. I'm really excited about the police ball. I have so many ideas for it. Did you know they've never actually had it at the Historical Thomas Center?" We start walking out of our apartment to Luca's car.

"What are you planning for it?"

"Oh my gosh. I'm absolutely going all out. They didn't give me much of a budget. But that's okay. I'm sure they have to spend their money on other things."

He gives me a look as we get in the car. "How are you going all out, then?"

"Well, most money gets spent on food. But a lot of times, you can get super great discounts on food if the event is for charity."

"That actually makes sense."

"For the police ball, though, a lot of people in the area support the department and its officers. I've already put some feelers out." I smile in excitement and bounce a little. "I'm going to have area grocery stores donate the food and..." I look at him hopefully.

He glances at me then back at the road, waiting for me to continue. I bite my lip and wait for him to catch on. I know he will. It just may take him a few moments. My smile brightens when he glances back at me.

His expression falls slightly. "Oh no. No, no, no. No. Lyric. Absolutely not."

I bounce a little more. "Please? Luca, you're an amazing chef. If I could get the food and the chef donated..."

"Lyric, no." He shakes his head. "I cook for you and me. That's it."

"And you're amazing. I know you love cooking. Almost as much as building things."

"I'm not doing it. Absolutely not happening."

I deflate slightly and play the card I hate playing. I only use it when I know I'm right, and he needs to concede. "Not even to help out your sister?"

"Oh. Come on, Lyric. Don't do that."

I look out the window as we near the Thomas Center. "It's okay. I'm sure I can find a chef." I sigh. "It just makes less of a budget for other things." I pat his thigh when he stops. "It's okay." I start to open my door and hide my smile. I know I have him.

He groans. "What do you want made?"

I look over and smile. "You'll do it?"

He puts up a finger. "On one condition."

"Name it." I squeak excitedly.

"I do not have to deal with dessert, and you do not make me cook pork or veal or lamb. They are notoriously difficult and not good for a huge crowd no matter what the fuck anyone says."

"That's two conditions, but done!" I hug him tightly. "Thank you! Thank you! Thank you!"

"You owe me. So much."

I kiss his cheek. "Anything!" I quickly get out of the car.

"You may regret that!"

I giggle as I skip into the building. The Police Officer's Grand Ball is going to be the event of the year. And perhaps the start of the career I've always dreamed of.

Chapter Two

⋆ *DJ* ⋆

I settle into a booth in the back corner of Panera Bread with my phone in my hand as I answer an email. My morning has been a little insane. Getting out of the office for a little while is the highlight of my entire day.

As soon as I put down my phone, it rings. I close my eyes as an explosion of pain starts in my neck and makes its way up into my head. I contemplate keeping my eyes closed and ignoring my phone, but even I know pretending it doesn't exist won't make it go away.

I sigh as I open my eyes and reach around to start rubbing the back of my neck. I pick up my phone with the other hand without looking at the caller ID. "Captain Rens," I growl.

I hear a chuckle on the other end. "Bad day, DJ?"

I smile. "Luca. If you're calling to cancel on me, I'm hunting you down. I fucking need a break. The broccoli and cheese bread bowl is calling my name."

He laughs. "I'm not. But I'm running late. Be about five minutes or so. I was calling to say go ahead and order."

My stomach growls. "I'll do it now. You want your usual?"

"Please."

"Done." I hang up as I stand and head for the register.

The girl behind the counter gives me a bright smile. Her blue eyes sparkle when she sees the badge on my belt and gun in my shoulder holster. As she checks me out, I take a second to do the same with her.

Her blond hair is up in a messy bun. Her uniform t-shirt clings to her curves and leaves nothing to the imagination. She's a small girl, probably close to a foot shorter than I am. I'm six feet three. Where I am very muscular, she is petite in every way. While it's pretty obvious to me that she's a badge bunny, she's definitely the type I'd hook up with.

The thought makes me chuckle a little. If I'm being honest, I'm probably old enough to be this girl's father. I'm fifty. She's probably in her early twenties. Judging from the way she's looking at me like she wants to devour me, though, I don't think she gives a fuck.

"What can I get you…" She trails off and looks down at my badge again. Her eyes linger. Her tongue slips out just enough to lick her lips. She smiles again and lets her eyes slowly make their way back up my body until she meets my eyes once more. "Captain?"

I give her a sexy, lopsided grin. "I'll take the broccoli cheese soup in a bread bowl with a chicken bacon ranch salad. Also throw a roasted turkey avocado BLT in there with a bowl of mac and cheese."

She bites her lip and looks down at the register. "That's a lot of food, Captain. Where do you plan to put it?"

I reward her with a laugh. "Mostly in my stomach, but I have a buddy coming. He'll eat the rest."

She giggles as she gives me my total. I hand her my credit card. When she gives it back, she lets her fingers brush against mine. I put my card away as the receipt prints. When she hands me a pen with the receipt, I quickly sign it and give her a wink when I give it back to her. She blushes and bites her lip again.

She looks up through her lashes. "When do you get done today?" she asks quietly.

I smile. "I work long hours. The way my day is going? Doubtful I'll be home before ten."

She pouts slightly. "Oh. Well, maybe if you need to blow off some steam…" She quickly writes something on a piece of scratch paper near her register. "Give me a call."

I take the scrap paper and make a show of glancing at it before slipping it in my pocket. "Are you telling me you're not going to be out partying tonight?" I give her a teasing smile.

She giggles again. "I don't spend a lot of time partying, Captain," she says as seriously as she can. "Unless I have the right partner."

I look up when I see my order being set on the counter. "I'll call you later. See what you're up to."

She smiles brightly and turns to the next customer who just walked in as I head for the counter. I take the tray and make my way to the table I've already saved. I set the tray down and grab the cups to fill our drinks.

Just after I settle, I see Luca walk in and scan the room for me. He smiles when he sees me and hurries over. He slides into the booth across from me and hungrily eyes the food I've set up for him.

"Fuck, I'm starving," he moans. He takes a bite of the sandwich and closes his eyes as he chews. After he swallows, he opens his eyes. "Sorry I'm late. Lyric had a hell of a nightmare last night. She woke up screaming. She hasn't done that in a while."

"Oh, shit. Is she okay?"

"Yeah. She bounced back and somehow managed to get me to agree to cook for that fucking police ball coming up."

I laugh. "Good. Put your skills to good use."

He shakes his head. "You both are relentless. You'd be perfect for each other, but if you touch my sister, I'll kill you." He tries to give me a stern look, but can't. He laughs instead.

Luca tries to be the tough, big brother, but he's been trying to set me up with his twin for a few months. I think some part of him thinks I'll be good for her or something. I've resisted every single meeting he's attempted to set up because I know better. I'm not good for anyone.

I'm far too much of a player for his sister. I've been married three times. They've all ended in divorce. Part of that is on my job. I'm a Captain with the Gainesville Police Department. I work long hours. I see things many people would never be able to deal with. And I see it on a daily basis. Dealing with Gainesville's scum takes a toll on a person. It takes a strong as hell woman to be with a cop. I have yet to find her. I've given up at this point in my life.

The other part is that I'm fully aware of how much of an asshole I am. Many say it's a defense mechanism. Push people away before they

15

hurt me. That kind of thing. Truth is, that's never been what it is with me. I'm really just a dick. At least that's how my controlling, protective, possessive, and dominant nature comes off to people.

It's sexy to women for a little while. Apparently, though, it gets old quickly. According to my last ex-wife, who I caught cheating on me with a cop from the county, I'm too much for her. She needs to spread her wings or some shit. Like I'd ever stop her from following her dreams. I'd never done anything but encourage her. I just didn't tolerate the sneaking around and lying. I guess wanting my wife to be faithful to me made me the bad guy.

The divorce papers listed irreconcilable differences as the cause for our split. I let it go because I wanted her out of my life. I planned to give her my house. I let her keep her car. Everything. I walked away with my clothes, and a few personal belongings.

It wasn't until she started spreading shit around about me being emotionally and mentally abusive towards her that I lost it and confronted her, through my attorney, of course. I'm not stupid. I've never been abusive to her or anyone in any manner. The extent of my controlling nature never crossed lines. I never told her she couldn't hang out with friends. I never kept her tied up at home.

That didn't stop her from making me out to be some kind of tyrant. Thank fuck the Judge saw through her bullshit. It didn't help her case that I had some nice photographic evidence of the indiscretion she said didn't happen. By the time it was all said and done, she ended up with nothing but her own personal belongings and the vehicle I bought for her. I paid it off the day my divorce was finalized and sent her on her way.

I moved back into my house and have thought very little of her since I watched her drive away. That was two years ago. I haven't looked back, but I was pretty fucked up over it. It's really just recently that I'm allowing myself to get back to the person I used to be. Apparently, that would be the asshole that's sexy to girls for a little while.

It's fine with me. I'm content with my life. I'll show a badge bunny a good time. I'll take her to bed. Then I'll send her on her way. They're happy to get their cop for a night. I'm happy to get off. I'm done with relationships. I don't have a good track record with them. Frankly, I don't care for them at this point in my life anyway.

Which is the entire reason I'm staying clear of Luca's sister. I value my friendship with him. He's a good guy. I hired the company he works for to do some work on my house. The day they were supposed to finish, I found out they were slightly behind schedule. They planned to come back and finish the next day. I couldn't fault them for the week-long rain delay they faced. I was pretty damn impressed they managed to catch up and stay that close to their original finish date.

Luca, though, decided to stay after everyone left and finish the work himself. There wasn't a lot left. Just a couple of windows in my den that needed to be installed. So, I rolled my sleeves up, and we finished it together. Afterwards, we shared dinner and a beer. Over the course of four hours, this thirty-year-old guy became one of my best friends.

"No work today?" I ask as we finish off our lunch.

"Nope. Day off. I need it. We just finished a house. I don't know why, but this one got to me physically. It's not like I've never carried sheets of wood or sheetrock, but fuck me. Yesterday, I sat in a bath of the hottest water I could stand. Pretty sure my flesh was being scalded, but it felt like fucking Heaven."

I raise an eyebrow. "Wonder if that's because you don't take days off."

He laughs. "The goal is to become a United States citizen. I can't do that if I don't make enough. It's expensive."

"Luca, I happen to know you make more than I do." I lean back after I finish my salad. "You have nothing to worry about. When do you take that test thing you were talking about?"

"Couple years still. I have to live here for a certain amount of time first. I don't care what I have to do, though. I'll do whatever I need to do if it means Lyric is safe."

I watch him for a few moments. "You ever going to tell me what happened?"

He looks down with a sigh and pushes the last of his sandwich around his plate. "It's not a happy story, man."

"I didn't figure it was. Most people don't flee their home country for the hell of it. Usually, something pretty bad has to happen in order for them to uproot everything they've ever known and run."

He smiles softly with a low chuckle as he shakes his head. "You'd never look at me the same."

I furrow my brows and cross my arms over my chest. "You know I won't push it, but you should also know that statement is bullshit. I'd never judge you."

He just nods, but his eyes don't meet mine. I've suspected for quite a while what happened. Usually, the reason people uproot their whole lives and move to another country is because they are running from something. Persecution. A crime.

Luca, on the other hand, is quite a lot like me. I know that he and Lyric are all each other has. I also know that she's always wanted to live in the United States. It's been her dream. But I'm also incredibly observant. Every time I bring up his citizenship and how close he is to getting it, Luca tends to go quiet on me.

I've come to the conclusion that they left the United Kingdom for a very good reason. But I know it's not just because it's Lyric's dream. I can tell there's far more to it than just that. Luca has told me of several nightmares Lyric has had. While they've lessened in frequency, they've increased exponentially in severity. Whatever the reason is that they left has to do with her.

"You know you can tell me, Luca. When you're ready, okay?" I look at my watch and groan.

He chuckles and finally meets my eyes again. His carefully guarded persona is back in place. "Big case?"

"Not exactly. At least not for me. But one of our investigators is hot on the trail of someone he thinks is involved in some gang. One of the key players. His partner is out sick today."

"I see. So, Captain Rens needs to fill in."

I laugh and shake my head. "I told him I'd do a stake-out with him. He's one of the newer investigators. He's got some good instincts. If he's right, it could be a good bust for him. And if it takes another bad guy off the streets and makes the city a little safer, I'm happy with that."

Luca looks at his phone and sighs. "Just as well. I need to head back to the Thomas Center and plan the menu. I really don't have a lot of time to prepare."

"Next weekend, right?"

"Huge menu. Giant task. I cook for two people. Not two thousand."

I laugh. "I say three fifty at the most."

He laughs. "I think I'll go with the expert on that one. You know. The girl who has the guest list and is actually planning the event."

I grin. "Probably for the best. I don't even know if I'm going."

"You have to go," a sickeningly sweet voice says next to me.

Luca and I look at each other before we both look up at the girl from the counter. I give her a sexy smile. "I should, huh? Why?"

"It's the police ball, right?" she asks.

I nod. "It is. How did you know that's what we were talking about?" I let my deep Southern accent do what it does best. People in Florida have a slight accent, but it's nothing to those of us from Texas. While I've been away from Texas for over thirty years, my accent has always remained.

"I was coming by to say my shift is over." She bites her lip. I watch her tongue flick across it and fight the urge to roll my eyes. I don't know when women started thinking that was the only thing they could do to make themselves seem sexy, but it's a very common move.

"And you overheard us?" I ask, already knowing the answer. I flick my eyes to Luca as he stifles a chuckle and starts to stand. I smile because he knows me well.

"Mmhmm. I hope I'm not being too presumptuous, but…" She bites her lip again. It's cute the first time. It gets fucking annoying really fast. "Maybe I can go with you."

Luca can't hold it back. He laughs. "Sorry, sweetheart. You lost him at the eavesdropping part." He winks at her. "He really fucking hates that."

I stand and clean up my mess. Luca gathers our garbage. I look down at her. "He's right. It's a pet peeve."

Her mouth falls open. "I wasn't! I swear. I just heard it on my way over!"

"Another pet peeve is when people lie to me." I let my voice drop as I narrow my eyes. She has the decency to lower hers. She knows she's been caught. I lean down so she can hear me whispering. "I saw you over by the soda machine. You've been there for the past ten minutes. Can't tell me it takes that long to clean up a little bit of a spill that never even made it to the floor."

She whimpers. "I -"

I reach in my pocket and pull out the paper she wrote her number on as I glance at her name tag. I take her hand in mine and put the paper in it. I close her hand around it. "Have a good day, Macy."

I follow Luca out the door, leaving Macy looking after us. I don't know if she's seething or crying, but I don't really care.

"Guess you'll have to find another cop chaser to fulfill your needs tonight," Luca laughs when we get outside.

I grin. "Your proper English is adorable, but we call them badge bunnies here."

He laughs again and shoves me when we get to my squad. "Such an asshole. Don't call me adorable again."

I raise an eyebrow and level him with a teasing grin. "Doesn't everyone fall for that accent?"

He looks at me deadpan. "Yeah. Women find it irresistible. You can stay the fuck away from me."

We both crack up as we say our goodbye. I head back for the station. I definitely needed that reprieve. Given what's on my plate for the rest of the day, Gainesville PD will be lucky if I don't quit by the end of night.

Chapter Three

☆ Lyric ☆

My Saturdays usually end up pretty busy. I guess it's a good thing I'm single because I don't think I've had a Saturday off since I started event planning. Tonight is a birthday party for one of Gainesville's police officers. But she has no idea it's happening. Her husband has been planning it for months behind her back as a surprise. Complete with music from the late nineties and early two-thousands.

I smile as I look over the playlist. "Janet Jackson. Mariah Carey. Spice Girls. Madonna." I laugh. "Backstreet Boys. Five. Boy bands galore!" I hand the playlist to the DJ. "Looks fantastic."

"Thank you, Ms. Sharpe. I have myself set up in the corner by the dance floor. I brought the strobe lights in case you change your mind about those."

I shake my head. "No. Not only do I hate them, but I have it on good authority that the birthday girl hates them more than I do. We'll stick with the laser lights. But not those strobe laser lights. You said you have some that are in the shape of butterflies?"

"Yes ma'am. I'll make sure to set those up."

I nod. "Perfect. If you need me, I'll be checking on the food in the kitchen. When you're all finished, come grab a plate. There's plenty. Just tell the cook I sent you back there to get something."

"Thank you, ma'am."

I smile as I head for the kitchen. I have been trying to keep my mind on the task at hand, but I keep thinking about the police ball. As I make my rounds, I envision the tables for the ball. The centerpieces. The live orchestra. Exactly how the silent auction will be set up. The colors of everything. I have planned everything down to the smallest detail. The police ball is always at the back of my mind.

My eyes widen as one of the servers begins walking past me with a plate full of delectable smelling hors d'oeuvre. Only I can see they are fish. Raw fish. And something that looks like sushi and caviar.

"No, no, no." I shake my head as I take the tray from her while I am still walking. "Nope. Absolutely not. Where did you get these?"

"Uh… The chef?" she squeaks as she follows me. "I was putting them in the spare refrigerator!"

I put the tray down on the prep table. My mouth drops at the massive amount of appetizers in front of me. "What is happening here? Did you not look at the menu?" I look up at the chef. She's an older woman with gray hair tied up in the tightest bun I've ever seen. She reminds me of my third-grade teacher. And she's just as frightening. I swallow when her eyes land on mine.

"Your appetizers are hardly upscale," she says. She turns her nose up.

I blink. "The birthday party girl doesn't like fish. Get rid of this. All of this. Immediately." I force the words out of my mouth, even though my heart is beating so quickly it might pop out of my chest and end up on the floor. I hate confrontation. Hate it.

She scoffs. "I will not. Just because she doesn't like it, doesn't mean others won't." She turns away from me.

I grip my chest and rub. "Oh my God," I whisper. I shake my head. "Excuse me, but I said no. She doesn't like fish. The smell makes her physically ill."

The chef turns towards me like she's been wounded. "How dare you not tell me that?"

My eyes widen even more. "I did! It's in your notes!" That's not something I'd ever fuck up.

"I can't work under these conditions!" She dramatically throws all of the appetizers and trays into the garbage.

I just stand and watch her throw her tantrum. She leaves the kitchen in a flourish. Her entire staff ignores everything that happened and continues cooking and doing whatever task they were assigned like nothing happened. I blink a few times as I sit down. I don't care that it's on the floor.

"Ms. Sharpe?"

I look up at a male with an accent I can't place. He's tall and well-built. His hair is flaming red. He's dressed like a chef, complete with a jacket and hat. For a moment, I honestly believe I'm dreaming. If not for the stabbing pain in my chest and the fact that I'm hyperventilating, I would choose to keep believing it.

Unfortunately, this is definitely my own personal living nightmare. "Yes?" I keep rubbing my chest, trying desperately to relieve the ache.

"It's okay. Really. She does that a lot. She tries to change the menu at the last minute and gets pissed when she's called out on it. I'll take care of it. I won't let that stuff go out. I've already prepped the honey barbecue chicken wings you asked for. I also have steak and chicken. I have the garlic mashed potatoes. I have the cream cheese ham and pickle wraps. I'm doing the deep-fried green olives with cream cheese. The only thing she refused to bring was the fruit for the fruit skewers, but I can send someone right now to get those."

The more he talks, the more relaxed I become. Instead of answering him, though, I leap to my feet and hug him. "You're a life-saver. Thank you."

He hugs me back and laughs. "You're welcome. We got this. Don't worry."

I pull away slowly with a nod and deep breath. "Okay. Good."

He holds me at arm's length. "You okay now?"

"Much. Thank you. What about the cake?"

He lets me go. "Cake is in the walk-in fridge. Chocolate covered strawberries are with it. I made those earlier."

"White chocolate?"

"Yes, ma'am."

I nod and relax even more. "Good. Good. Okay." I nod again and take one more look around before looking at my watch. I bite my lip. "Thirty minutes until guests arrive. Please tell me you can fix all of this."

"Already being fixed. You go do what you need to do. We'll deal with this." And with that, he's off like a whirlwind.

I take another breath and scrub my hands down my face before going back to the party room. I see my boss walking through the room and looking at all of my magenta balloons and different shades of pink confetti. I bite at my lip nervously as I watch her take in the fire and ice carnation centerpieces.

"Oh. Lyric," she says when she spots me. "I saw the chef leave. Is everything okay?"

I throw on a fake smile I hope looks confident and sincere. "Absolutely, Ms. Kelly. She was not happy about the menu. She had fish. A lot of fish. Our guest doesn't like fish. It makes her sick. I specifically put that in her instructions, but she informed me the menu wasn't elegant enough for her. Her sous chef is taking care of things from here. Everything looks amazing."

Kelly makes a disgusted face. "Remind me to take her off of our list of suggested caterers. But keep the sous chef."

"I definitely will." I take out my phone and quickly email her. "Emailing to you now."

"I love how efficient you are, Lyric. You're doing fantastic. Everything looks incredible. I would never know those carnations aren't real if I hadn't seen you making them." She smiles and pats me on the back lightly as she leaves the room.

I breathe a sigh of relief at both her praise and the fact that she likes my work. I would never tell her the reason I am so efficient in emailing her things right away or making lists is because I have issues remembering things sometimes. It's a side-effect of my past. A past I want nothing more than to forget in the same way I do so many other things. I intentionally shake my head to rid my mind of the images threatening to make their way into my memory. I refuse to let myself go there. I won't.

After I finish with the last-minute touches, it's time. Guests begin to arrive. I move to a corner where I can see everything and admire my work. One of my favorite things is seeing the reaction on the faces of people when they see the decor and painstaking details I put into planning. It makes me happy when my guests are happy.

I furrow my brows when I see my brother walk in with someone, but I stay in my corner until it's time for the guest of honor to enter. I hurry to the DJ to get him to quiet everyone. Matt Chance, the birthday girl's husband, said they'd be arriving at exactly six o'clock. It's five minutes to.

"Ready to silence the crowd?" I ask with a bright smile.

"Ready when you are."

"It's time. We have a couple of minutes. I'll get the lights."

"I'll silence the people."

I smile again as I head for the doors where the lights are. I wait for the DJ to do his thing. Everyone gathers together. I shut the lights out when everyone is ready. I shiver in anticipation. I can't wait to see Matt's wife's face. I bite my lip in anticipation as the doors to the room open slowly.

"Come on, Matt. I want to see where we are," a soft female voice says as the door opens. It must be Mariah. I bounce on my toes and wait for Matt to remove his hands from her eyes.

"Patience, beautiful. Stand right here…" He positions her in front of him as he quietly closes the door to the room. "Ready?"

"More than ready. Matt, let me see!"

"Okay. Hand is off your eyes," he says.

I silently thank him for that because it's dark in here. I can't see him remove his hand. I flip on the lights and pull the lever for the confetti to drop from the ceiling. Matt said Mariah loves glitter. He, thankfully, vetoed any use of glitter, but did settle for a glittery type of pink confetti. Much easier to clean up, and it won't be on everyone and in everything for years to come.

"Surprise!" everyone in the room yells in unison.

I smile happily at Mariah's expression of pure surprise and bliss at everyone in the room here for her. She looks up as the glittery confetti falls. She holds her arms out and spins in a slow circle. She closes her eyes and lets her head fall back as she giggles and laughs. Matt watches her with such adoration, it makes me wish I had someone who looks at me the way he's looking at her. It's so adorable.

Matt turns and winks at me before he leads his incredibly beautiful wife to their table. The same one my brother is sitting at with his friend. Something interesting to discuss with Luca later. Right now, though, I decide it's the perfect time to take a break. The guests are mingling. The staff is bringing out appetizers.

I quietly slip away and disappear down a short hall off the room to the bathroom. When I finish, I take a few minutes to make sure my hair is still in place. I check my black slacks for any stray lint and make sure my white button-down shirt is perfect. I love this shirt. The sleeves go three-quarters of the way down my arm, so I'm not hot when I wear it. It also hugs my curves, but doesn't make me feel self-conscious. I can button it up enough so I don't feel like my boobs are popping out but also don't feel like I'm choking.

Satisfied I still look professional, I slip quietly out of the bathroom only to run directly into what feels like a steel wall. Before I understand what's happening, I'm on my ass staring up at the most beautiful man I have ever seen in my life.

He's tall. And not just because I'm sitting on the floor. He has to be well over six feet. He has short brown hair that's perfectly spiked. I'd wonder how much time he spent on it and how much money he spends on hair products, but I honestly think he just rolls out of bed and looks like a God. I don't think he tries at all.

His jeans fit every inch of him to perfection. His dark blue t-shirt leaves nothing about his physique to the imagination. I am almost certain his muscles have muscles. Everything, even his strong jawline, says to me that he was chiseled from something far stronger than titanium.

And his eyes. Good God. I could drown in them and die happy. I don't know if it's the light, or if he really does have a dark, deep jade eye color. I've never seen anything like them. They remind me a little of those really pretty marbles that come in that marble game.

There is no denying the man in front of me is gorgeous. As he kneels in front of me, I'm convinced that he's not only moving in slow motion, but that he's also got some kind of crazy golden aura around him. Like in the movies when they are being obnoxious and using that golden glow to highlight whoever it is that they want the lead character to fall in love with.

He holds out a hand. "You okay? I tried to catch you, but I couldn't turn fast enough."

I slowly and a little shakily take his hand. "Um... I... think... so." I try to tell myself to stop staring at him, but as he pulls me up with him, I can't make myself follow the directions my brain is screaming at me.

"I'm DJ." He keeps my hands in his as he turns me a little bit and looks me over.

"I'm... Lyric." I force myself to breathe. I shake my head a little bit as he turns me the other way and looks me over again. I chuckle a little. "I figured I'd get a cheesy pick up line or something before you started checking me out."

I'm rewarded with what I can only describe as a megawatt smile. "You mean something like... Are you a parking ticket? Because you've got *fine* written all over you."

I blink at him. "Really? That's the best you got?"

He laughs. "How about this one? Well, here I am. What are your other two wishes?"

I shake my head. "Um... For you to have better pick-up lines would be the first one. The second one would be a do-over. You know, not falling on my ass after running into your back."

He laughs again. "Alright. Here. How about this one? Did it hurt?"

I tilt my head. "Did what hurt? The fall?"

He gets a gleam in his eye. "When you fell from Heaven?"

I narrow my eyes, playfully. "Did you just call me Satan?"

He cracks up as he lets go of my hands, seemingly satisfied that I'm not hurt. I immediately miss the warmth. "Alright. Here's the best I got. Ready for it?"

"Lay it on me."

"Aside from being sexy, what do you do for a living?"

I suck my lower lip into my mouth to keep from laughing as I shake my head. "You're getting there. You should probably work on them more."

"Really? I dug deep for that one." He gives me a panty-soaking half-smile. "Okay. Okay. One more. But this one is from way back in the deep depths in the back of my mind."

"I'm waiting..."

"If you were a Transformer..." He pauses for dramatic effect before grinning. "You'd be Optimus *Fine*."

My lip quivers, but I can't stop the giggle that bubbles up. Before I can stop it, I'm laughing. "Those lines are so bad! Does anyone actually fall for those?"

"Jesus fuck, I hope not. I'd seriously question the woman's mentality and my own if I ever dropped one of those lines and it was fallen for."

"Thank God. My entire image of you would be completely ruined." My eyes immediately widen when I realize what I said. I put a hand over my mouth. "I…" I lower my eyes shyly.

DJ grins again. "Oh… she has an image of me…," he teases. "Hopefully, it's a big, strong gladiator type of man with a giant shield and sharp sword."

I giggle again, thankful to him for lightening the mood. I let my hand fall to my side as I look up at him. I smile. "Nope. It's a scrawny, nerdy guy who is trying to harness the Force," I tease.

He laughs. I love his laugh. It's deep and smooth. It rumbles through my entire body. "I'm fucking wounded." He grips his chest as he smiles. "Alright. You win. Give me your phone." He holds out his hand.

I raise an eyebrow, but do what he says. It's impossible not to obey his deep and commanding voice. "Why?" I hand him my phone after unlocking it.

"Because something is wrong with mine." He smiles and starts typing something.

I tilt my head. "What's wrong with yours?"

His smile turns into a grin as he hands me my phone back. "It didn't have your number in it. It's fine now. I fixed it." He winks as I take my phone.

I watch him as he walks away. It takes me a second to realize what he just did. "What an outrageous pick up line!" I start laughing when I look down at the text he sent himself from my phone. "Really? Hey, handsome?" I laugh again as he sits down at the table next to my brother.

It's then I realize he's the one who came in with Luca. Luca must also know Matt and Mariah because he seems just as friendly with them as he is with DJ. I lean against the wall as I watch their table. That must be the DJ that Luca is friends with. I'd never met him or really cared to. I've been too busy with work and trying to forget my past.

That might just have to change, though. I sincerely doubt I'll be getting DJ's eyes, or anything else about him, out of my head anytime soon. I glance down at the text he sent himself once more and smile. I feel butterflies take flight in my stomach, and a very odd warm feeling consumes me.

Well, DJ. I might just have to get to know you a little better, huh?

Chapter Four

★ *DJ* ★

(Two Days Later)

I let out a frustrated sigh as the officer I was just speaking with leaves my office. Not because of him. He was just the bearer of my bad mood. I might have to apologize with coffee and a donut tomorrow.

I lean back in my chair and scrub my hands down my face. "I'm in trouble. A lot of fucking trouble."

Trouble because I can't get a pair of hauntingly beautiful hazel eyes out of my mind. Lyric Sharpe. There was a reason I avoided meeting her. Several, actually. The most important being I'm not good for her. She's twenty years younger than me. From everything Luca has told me about her, she's had a fuck of a life. She needs someone to take care of her. She needs a man who will be there for her.

I am absolutely not him. I work long hours. I like having the ability to send my conquest of the night home when I'm through with her. I am perfectly content not seeing her again and continuing with my life. I've tried the relationship thing. They've all failed epically. I'm not in a hurry to start another one.

I growl low at a knock on my door. "What?"

Matt Chance, a Lieutenant with Gainesville Police Department and my best friend, opens my door and closes it behind him. "What's the matter with you? Timmons just stopped me and said to steer clear of you." He sits on one of the leather chairs in front of my desk.

"Obviously, you didn't listen."

"Do I ever?" He puts his feet up on my desk and crosses his arms over his chest. "So? What's up?"

Matt is a little taller than me. He's just as muscular. He has short dark brown hair and a little bit of scruff on his face to match his dark brown eyes. Tattoos cover his arms. Most people are intimidated by him. I can't blame them. They're intimidated by me, too. But it's one of the reasons I get along so well with him. Matt doesn't take shit from anyone. He's straight to the point. He doesn't fuck around. He's not only one of the best cops I've ever had the pleasure of working with, he's also an all-around good person.

I sigh and lean forward on my elbows. "Remember the other day at Mariah's party when we had Luca sitting with us? I told him I'd just met his sister, and the fucker started laughing?"

Matt raises an eyebrow. "Yeah?"

"Remember when he said it's about time, and that I should have just listened to him and met her earlier?"

"Yeah?"

"He's been trying to set me up with her for quite a while. I've been avoiding it."

Matt is silent for a few moments before he finally clears his throat. "Does this have to do with the fact that she's your friend's sister, and you don't want to fuck up your relationship with him? Or is it more that you still don't think you're relationship material?"

I hate that this asshole can see right through me. I lean back in my chair and mimic his position. I put my feet on my desk and cross my arms over my chest. "Both."

"Well, you know what I'm going to say, don't you?"

"Something ridiculous about how you felt the same way until Mariah came in and knocked you on your ass?"

He shrugs. "Love is love, man. And I'll be honest. I've known you a long fucking time. I've been here for you through two of your three marriages. I've been your support through your failed engagement. So, I think I've earned the right to say this. I've never seen you like this. With any of them, DJ. You're smitten with this one."

I glare at him. "Why am I friends with you?"

He has the audacity to grin. "Because I'm honest. I tell you straight. I don't hold back."

"Because you're an asshole."

He shrugs again and drops his feet. He stands. "That, too. You want my advice?"

"Nope."

"Call her."

"I said I didn't want your advice." My lip twitches. I try not to smile, but a half one comes out anyway.

Matt grins. "Call her." He closes my door behind him as he leaves.

"Asshole." I let out a long breath and look down at my phone.

Lyric has texted a couple of times. I haven't responded. It makes me feel like a jerk. Something else that is different about this entire thing with her. It's not like I've never responded to a call or text before. I've ghosted a lot of women I didn't want anything to do with. Not once have I felt like a dick because of it.

I don't know why the thought of doing it to her makes my heart hurt. I never should have given the girl my number. That was mistake number three thousand in a long list of them with her. Talking to her was the first one.

I scrub my hands down my face for the thousandth time today and jump when my phone vibrates. I glance down at it. Another text message. From her. I know I shouldn't read it, but I do because I'm obviously a glutton for torture.

Lyric: I know this is a long shot... You are probably really busy, but I was wondering if maybe you'd be going to the police ball this weekend? I thought perhaps I could see you...

I sigh again. I really need to say something to her. I know I do. Not saying anything is probably hurting her. Hurting her isn't something I want to do. The fact that I care about her feelings at all pisses me off.

DJ: Hey, Lyric. I apologize for not getting back to you sooner. I've been busy. Look, I probably shouldn't have given you my

number. I'm friends with your brother. I don't want to fuck that up. I'm also not relationship material. I don't want to hurt you.

Before I can change my mind, I quickly hit send. As soon as I do it, though, my heart starts pounding. I shut my phone off and toss it on the desk. Nausea immediately takes over. Stomach bile rises up my throat. I wonder if there's a way to unsend a text message after it's sent. I have half a mind to take it to my tech guys in the department. I probably would if it wouldn't mean explaining my reasoning.

"Fucking hell." I drop my feet and lean forward. I just need to throw myself into work and forget completely about Lyric.

But even I know that doesn't have a chance in all of creation of happening. Lyric is sweet. She's the kind of girl a man would want to take home to his family. She's got a biting sense of humor. I can tell she's incredibly shy, but she's still a strong woman. She's a natural fucking submissive. Perfect for me. No matter how hard I try, I can't stop the niggling voice in the back of my head that keeps telling me she's the type of woman who would make one fuck of a cop's wife.

She's also fucking gorgeous. She's really a small girl. She's close to a foot shorter than I am. I honestly think she could gain a few pounds, but I know from Luca that she's lost a lot of weight after whatever it was that happened to her. Stress can do some fucked up things to a person. Even still, it hasn't stopped me from thinking of all the things I'd like her to do with those sexy, pouty lips while I'm tangling my fingers in that slightly longer than shoulder length auburn hair.

It's those damn eyes I keep going back to, though. I could drown in them if she'd let me. They're so unique. I classify them as hazel, but it's only because there are so many different colors that I can't decide what they actually are. At first glance, I'd say brown. Then when the light hits them right, they look green. But when I stared at them longer, they almost looked golden. I don't think she realizes just how beautiful she is.

I don't know how much time has passed, but I've managed to lose myself in work at least enough so Lyric isn't on my mind. At least not as prevalently as she has been since two days ago at Mariah's party.

Of course, luck isn't on my side. I know I'm in for it when Mariah, Matt's wife and a police officer with Gainesville PD, slams my office door open. I jump and look up at her, my heart leaping into my throat.

I groan. The girl looks like the fucking angel of death. Or some dark witch, complete with her hair blowing around her face and sparks crackling in the air. I expect fire to shoot from her fingertips. She walks into my office and slams the door. Her ridiculously blue eyes look a little like ice when she lays a glare of the ages at me.

I hold up a hand. "Don't start."

She crosses to my desk and folds her arms over her chest. The cold death stare she's giving me turns impossibly frigid. "Are you actually crazy? Or is this just some stupidly obnoxious way to keep everyone at arm's length?"

I raise an eyebrow and lean back in my chair. "You're going to have to be a little more specific, gorgeous. I've pissed off a lot of people today."

"Ironic how the one person who should be pissed is far from it! I haven't known Lyric for long. I literally just met her at my party. But she is the sweetest, kindest person I have ever met in my entire life, DJ. And she doesn't deserve your bullshit excuses!"

I stand angrily. But more at myself than her. "Do you honestly think I don't know that? Why the fuck do you think I sent the fucking text in the first place?"

"Because you're a conceited, egotistical jackass who wouldn't know a good fucking thing if it came up and bit you in the fucking ass, maybe? Of all people you'd do this to, why her?"

"Mariah, I don't know how the hell you know what happened, but it doesn't involve you. Let it fucking go!"

Her mouth drops. Of all the women I've come across in the world, she has the ability to strike the fear of God into me. More than even my mother had before she passed away. Mariah is a fucking terrifying woman when she wants to be. I typically strive to stay on her good side. Apparently though, today I've managed to piss her off, too. Too bad, because Mariah is also one of my best friends.

"Because I was at lunch with her when you sent that text, you asshole! How could you do that? Why would you be stupid enough to give the girl your number only to be a complete douche and tear her down like that?"

I don't get a chance to respond before my door opens again. I give an exasperated sigh as Matt closes the door behind him. He gives me a glare to rival Mariah's as he crosses his arms over his chest.

"Oh, here we go." I sigh and shake my head as I sit back down.

"I said talk to her. I didn't say send her a fucking text that broke her heart." Matt stares me down as he towers over his seething wife.

"Stop it. Both of you," I warn. I'm not in the mood for either of them. Mariah said it herself. Lyric wasn't angry. She should know. She was with her.

Matt raises an eyebrow. "Stop it? Really? No. This right here is a motherfucking intervention. I've stood by long enough letting you think you're not good enough for any woman. Just because your bitch exes couldn't handle you and your job doesn't mean for a second that you aren't a good person. What the hell is wrong with you?"

"Matt. For the love of Christ, drop it!" I look up at him. "I'm not going to ruin her! She's too…" I pause trying to think of the right word. "She's everything I'm not. She's sweet. She deserves far better than some guy who doesn't care about anything more than his job or where he's getting his next lay! Fucking let it go! Both of you! Out of my office!"

Of course, neither of them listens to me. I can intimidate most anyone into doing what I want. But not these two. It's one of the reasons I get along with them so well. They stand up to me and have a tendency to put me in my place when I need to be.

But this is not one of those times. I know Lyric is better off without me. And I am fully aware that I fucked up when I gave her my number and flirted with her. I don't need either of them to tell me that.

"Fix this, DJ," Mariah growls at me. "I will not allow you to break her. She's been through enough shit in her life. She didn't deserve the tears you caused. She didn't deserve the doubt you've placed in her mind. Or the pain." The viciousness makes me jump slightly. "I never thought I would ever be ashamed to call you my best friend. I never thought you could be so callous. Looks like I was wrong."

"Do not let that girl walk away from you. She could be everything you've ever dreamed of." Matt levels me with one more glare before he grabs Mariah's arm and steers her out of my office.

It's probably a good thing. She looked like she wanted to kill me. If Matt hadn't steered her out when he had, it's highly likely she would have jumped over my desk and started strangling me.

Although, why is slightly beyond me. She's the one who said Lyric wasn't pissed. It would stand to reason that she's okay. She probably even agreed with me. I'm sure she's smart enough to see right through the likes of me and didn't want anything to do with me or my game. I'd never blame her for that.

Though, the words she uttered after that have my heart in my throat. Pain? Tears? Doubt? What the fuck was that all about? Wouldn't it stand to reason she'd be fucking as pissed as they are at me if she was upset enough to cry?

I groan and drop my head in my arms on my desk. I can't get her out of my mind. Ever since I saw her on Saturday, she's been all I can think about. It's so stupidly unlike me. I've never reacted like this to anyone. Not any of the women I married. None that I've been in a serious relationship with.

I've never ended up with an immediate hard on just at the thought of a woman's touch. And I've certainly never in my life thought about tangling my hands in a woman's hair and almost instantly coming. Not to say I've never thought of a girl between my legs getting me off. I'm not at all innocent. But I usually have to think of them doing something in order to get to that point. Never has just the silky feel of her hair brought me to a point of near no return.

I toss the pen I didn't know I was holding in disgust with myself and glance down at my phone for the millionth time since I shut it off hours ago. I finally give in and turn it on. When a text notification comes up, my heart leaps into my throat. My stomach clenches. I may actually stop breathing, but I force myself to stop acting like an idiot as I open the text. Just seeing Lyric's name does things to me it shouldn't.

Lyric: Oh... Okay... I'm sorry... I didn't mean to bother you... I won't text you again...

My fingers hover over the keyboard as I try to decipher the text. The rational part of me is saying she's okay. But my heart is telling me she's a long way from it. I want to tell her she isn't a bother. That it's my fault for leading her on and making her think I could potentially be a good fit in her life. I want to tell her that she deserves far better than a man like me.

But I can't bring myself to do it. I can't force my fingers to punch in the letters to formulate the words that I want to say to her. I don't want to hurt her any more than I already did if that's what's going on here. The best thing to do is leave it alone. Just like I originally planned.

Giving up on the day, I grab my gear and shut my computer down. I have a lot of shit to do, but I can't concentrate on any of it. There isn't a point sitting here suffering any more than I have to. I glance at my watch as I walk out to the garage where my personal vehicle is parked.

I love my Mustang. Brand new. Convertible. Leather interior that always has that brand new smell. My car is my pride and joy. She's been the only partner I've had in my life that hasn't betrayed me. And the best thing about her is she doesn't say a fucking word. Even if I'm the one in the wrong. She just purrs under me and listens to me if I decide to talk. She's the only woman in my life, other than Mariah, who hasn't turned on me.

Well, I can't say Mariah hasn't at this point. Her disappointment in me breaks my cold exterior just a little.

Which, of course, brings my thoughts right back to Lyric as I slide into the driver's seat. I growl low as I start the car. "I get the feeling I really fucked this up."

As if the universe agrees with that statement, the radio starts playing something about someone who got away. I look at the dash incredulously as I leave the garage. Not believing in soulmates and happy endings. Someone sneaking up and making the world better. I quickly turn the radio off.

Apparently, Satan isn't done fucking with me, though. As I'm driving, I see a giant billboard advertising events at the Historical Thomas Center. It, of course, makes me think immediately of Lyric. An advertisement on a bus as I drive past has confetti. I think of the party. Which, in turn, makes me think of Lyric.

I growl as I stop at a red light. At the corner, waiting to cross, is a small, dark haired woman wearing black slacks and a white button-down shirt. She's looking down at her phone. She glances up at me before she hurriedly starts crossing the street.

My face scrunches in horror and even a little anger because I start thinking of Lyric. "Are you fucking kidding me?"

When the light turns green, I make a beeline for downtown. I glance at the clock on my dash. It's almost six. Perfect time for the popular bars to start filling up. It's exactly what I need. Someone blonde. And tall. Exactly the opposite of Lyric.

Because if I keep thinking of her, she's going to break me like no other woman has ever had the power of doing before.

No.

I need to get back into my routine.

A routine that doesn't involve Lyric Sharpe.

Chapter Five

✦ Lyric ✦

My body feels a little like a blanket of lead is over me. I couldn't move even if I wanted to. Which I don't. I don't ever want to move again. I'm too weak to even cry anymore. I really don't even feel Luca's fingers running through my hair. If he didn't shift every now and again, I'm not sure I'd even know he's here.

Even though his stomach is literally in front of my face. I've been laying here in his lap with my head facing his stomach ever since Mariah dropped me off after lunch earlier. I was barely aware Luca even got home. If it hadn't been for the change in scent when he sat down and settled my head on his lap, I probably would still think Mariah is here.

I grip the fleece blanket tight and inhale Luca's fresh, after the rain, and slightly spicy scent. Warm. Comforting. Home. Like the one place in the world I always know I'm safe. I close my eyes once more and grip the hem of Luca's shirt with my other hand. I tuck both of my hands underneath my chin and curl into myself even more than I had been. I tuck my knees closer to my chest as the tears begin falling silently once more.

How? I don't know. I thought I was all cried out.

I tremble. "Why doesn't he want me?" I whisper. I don't expect Luca to answer. I don't even think he hears me. It's not until his deep voice rumbles that I realize I spoke out loud.

"Lyric. You can't do this to yourself," he says quietly. He tugs my hair gently.

I burrow even more, though, I'm not certain it's possible. "I thought he liked me. Why doesn't he like me anymore? Did I do something wrong?"

"DJ is the one who did something wrong, Lyric. Not you."

"But why? What did I do to make him not want me?" I tremble even more.

"Nothing. You didn't do anything."

"Maybe I texted him too much." I think of the couple of messages I sent him. He never responded to the first one. Maybe I shouldn't have sent the second one. Or the third. Or fourth. "I bothered him too much."

"You didn't, sis. You didn't do anything wrong. This isn't your fault. It's his. He's afraid he's not good enough for you. And he's fucking bloody right."

His growl makes me bite down on my lip hard enough to make it bleed. But even the metallic taste suddenly in my mouth doesn't make me let go. I squeeze my eyes closed as my heart beats erratically. I feel like I'm having a heart attack. A sob escapes my throat before I have a chance to stop it. Luca's t-shirt is soaked, but I can't stop the waterfall pouring from my eyes.

I should have known that someone like DJ wouldn't be interested in someone like me. He seems like such a great person. He can have any woman he wants in this entire world. I should have known that he'd never want someone as damaged as I am. He said that he isn't relationship material. I'm not an idiot. That's just a nice way of saying he doesn't want me.

I can't blame him. And I don't. I don't blame him for wanting to steer clear of someone like me. I know I'm not who he usually dates. I've heard about him. At least a little. Mariah even told me some about him at lunch today before he sent that text. A man like him would never be satisfied with one woman. Especially a quiet, shy, mousy type of woman like me.

DJ likes more flashy women. Pretty. Flirty. I'm too introverted. Nobody likes a woman who has no confidence in herself. Someone who needs constant reassurance that she's good enough. Who is too clingy and needy.

That must have been what it was. I must have come off too needy. I bothered him with the texts too much. I should have waited for him to text me. And more than just the cute text he sent himself to get my number. I should have waited for him to say something.

Instead, I was too stupid and bugged him. I was too eager to get to know him. I should have known I wasn't good enough for him. I never should have gotten my hopes up. I knew when I was talking to him that I wasn't enough for him. But I let myself think that just maybe he wouldn't pull the rug out from under me.

This entire thing is completely my fault. It's my fault for looking at DJ's devilish smile as a crack of sunlight in the darkness that is my world. I should have stayed hidden in the shadows where I belong. Someone like me doesn't belong in the light DJ casts. I don't belong in his universe. It was a mistake to think for a second I could compete with the women he's used to.

I shouldn't have been so dumb. Thinking I had a chance with someone like him was so, so idiotic on my part. I've never been enough for anyone before. There's so much wrong with me. I have so many flaws.

I know I'm not pretty enough. I'm too skinny or too fat. I've never been perfect. My hair isn't as long as men like. It's an ugly brown. My eyes don't sparkle and shine. My skin doesn't glow. I'm short. I'm not that perfect height men like. My tits are too big. They're disproportionate to the rest of me. Even a man with large hands can't just grip them and have them fit into his palm. I don't have that perky ass men love to grab a hold of.

I jump nearly a mile at the knock on the door. I look up at Luca wide-eyed, silently begging him to both not let me go and make whoever is on the other side of the door go away. He looks at the door with a sigh as I tremble. I whimper when he gets up. I cling to him because that's what I do. Too clingy.

"It's okay. I promise," he whispers as he gently untangles my fingers from his shirt.

I sit up and watch him as I uncontrollably shiver. I grip the edge of the blanket and wrap myself tighter into it as I try to disappear into the back of the couch. Tears still fall from my eyes, but I'm too exhausted to make a sound. I can barely feel anything. Instead, I bury my face in the back of the couch and pull the blanket up higher so it's covering most of my face. Only one eye and the top of my head is showing. I subtly wipe my eyes. Unless someone is really paying attention, they'd never know.

"How is she?" someone asks quietly. A male, but I don't care enough to open my eyes to see who it is.

"Not well. She's blaming herself," Luca says. "It's typical. When something out of her control happens, her mind finds a way to make her think it's her fault."

"Because it is," I whisper. I feel someone sit next to me, but it's not Luca. Before I have a chance to give in and open my eyes, I'm being tugged against a solid and warm body. I squawk and flail as I open my eyes to meet Matt's.

"Lyric." His voice is deep and startlingly commanding. "None of this is your fault. None of it." He wraps his strong and comforting arms around me as he looks at me.

I don't know Matt well. I know him mostly from planning Mariah's party, but he's become one of my favorite people. I hit it off with him fairly quickly. Though not as quickly as I did with Mariah. I've only known her a couple of days and already she's probably my best friend. She's kind and genuine. And she didn't leave me after she brought me home today. Not until she was forced to, but that wasn't until Luca was home, and she was sure I was going to be okay.

At least relatively.

Matt, however, has already seen me at my worst. And he sat with me the entire time. Just after we met, I'd had a panic attack over a pipe bursting in the room we planned to hold Mariah's party. Water started pouring into the room from the ceiling. I had no idea what to do, but it wasn't because of that. It was because it reminded me of something that had happened to me.

Other than Luca, Matt is the only one who knows about it. I had to tell him something because I was clinging to him and bawling like a toddler into his shoulder as he held me. Protected me. Kept my demons away.

And just like that day, I find myself curled into Matt like he's the only thing keeping me from flying into space. I squeeze my eyes closed once more and keep the blanket as high on my face as possible. He says it isn't my fault, but I know better. If I wasn't the way I am, DJ wouldn't have said what he did.

"You going to be okay?" Luca asks. I don't have time to ask what he means before Matt speaks.

"I got her. Go deal with him."

I jump and twist myself towards Luca. "Luca, no! Don't!" I squeak. Images of the last time he got involved in one of my relationships comes flooding back to me so hard I clutch my chest because I can't breathe. I try to reach for him, but I get tangled in the blanket that, just a few minutes ago, I considered security. I struggle to get loose.

Matt grips me in a vice-like hold I have no chance of getting out of. "Stop." He holds me closer. "Lyric! Stop!"

I obey, but I'm hyperventilating. "Luca, don't!" I am full-on sobbing, but I don't care. "Please, please don't!"

"Lyric, I'm not going to hurt him. Okay? I promise. It's not going to be like before."

I hiccup and squeak as I cry. Matt hugs me as close as he possibly can. But all I can think of is Luca's knuckles bloodied as he stands over a bleeding and busted up DJ. I want to believe him when he says it's not going to happen like that again, but the images won't go away.

He leans over and hugs me. He kisses my cheek. I know he's trying to comfort me, but it's no comfort. I know what Luca is capable of when someone hurts me. I've seen it first-hand. It's one of the reasons we left the United Kingdom.

I know I'm not going to be able to stop Luca from confronting DJ. So, while my heart beats so quickly that it sounds like a jet plane to me, I turn back into Matt and grip his shirt as I bury my face in his neck. His strong, spicy scent is just as calming as Luca's fresh rain one is.

✮✮✮

"Lyric. Explain to me why you think this is your fault in the least. Because I'm struggling trying to figure that one out," Matt asks after Luca has long since left. I've finally calmed down enough to not be sobbing. Matt hasn't let me go the entire time.

I'm quiet for a long moment before I finally take a breath. "Where's Mariah?" I whisper.

He soothingly runs one hand up and down my back while he runs his other one through my hair. "Working. She got tied up on a call. Now, answer my question, please."

I bite my lip and stay silent for another long while. I know Matt well enough to know he won't drop it. He made me tell him why I freaked out when the pipe burst. He wouldn't let it go until I finally opened up to him. I know he won't judge me. He didn't then.

"Because I was too eager. Too…" I trail off, trying to think of the right words. "Too clingy. I texted him too much. I should have waited until he messaged me first."

Matt shakes his head and tugs my hair just hard enough so I look up at him, but not hard enough to hurt me. "I have never seen DJ react to anyone the way he did to you, Lyric. DJ is… complicated. He's been through a lot of shit in relationships. He has it in his beyond thick and very stupid skull that he isn't relationship material. That isn't your fault."

"But… I pushed him," I whisper as I look down.

Matt dips his head. He tugs my hair again so I have to look at him. "You didn't do anything wrong. It isn't your fault that DJ got spooked over his feelings for you."

I shake my head. "I feel like…" I sigh. "He just seemed so different, Matt. I feel like I just dug into him with both hands and clung hard with both feet. I scared him. And that is my fault. It was so wrong of me. I guess I just wanted to believe that not all guys were the same as the ones I've been with." I lower my eyes. "I was too eager. I can't imagine how uncomfortable I made him feel. I'm such an idiot. And I'm not anywhere near the women he must be used to."

"My God, Lyric. Honey, you really don't know how special you are, do you?"

I look up at him once more before sniffling and shifting to burrow myself back into him. Where I'm safe. Where my secrets are guarded. Where he can't see into my soul like he has a strange habit of being able to do.

"I'm not." I shake my head and close my eyes again. I grip his shirt tighter and try to focus on his heartbeat to steady my own.

"You're right, you know. At least partially. You aren't like the women DJ is used to. DJ is used to quick fucks. Women who are content having a cop on top of them for a night and going home in the morning. You aren't like that. You're a steady woman. Someone a man would be proud to have by his side and could never get enough of."

I blush and hide. "I'm not any of that."

"You are. And I'm not going to tolerate you thinking you aren't. You're an amazing woman, Lyric. I should know. Because Mariah has taken one hell of a liking to you. And she doesn't like anyone. It takes a lot for her to come home and tell me that she believes she found a friend. My wife has two friends other than me, Lyric. DJ is one of them. You're the other. So, when we went home the night of her party and she told me that she could really get to like Luca and that she thinks you're incredible, it speaks volumes about the type of person you are. And above and beyond that, I consider you one of my friends. I don't have many of those."

"I… just don't… understand what happened. If it's not because of something I did, then why would he tell me he shouldn't have given me his number?"

"Because he's scared."

I say nothing. Instead, I concentrate on the steady rhythm of his heart. I silently thank him for not pushing me further. I want to believe him when he says that DJ is scared. That it's not my fault. I tell myself over and over that it doesn't have to do with me. I try to convince myself that DJ is just being an asshole. I even tell myself that I'm better than him and don't deserve the way he treated me.

But the truth is, I can't convince myself of any of it. I still feel like I did something to cause him to tell me he didn't want anything to do with me. When I first read the text he sent, I tried to take it at face value. I told myself that he just values his friendship with my brother and doesn't want to lose that if something happened between us. I understand not wanting to cause a rift.

I even tried to believe him when he said he's not relationship material and doesn't want to hurt me. But as the minutes tick by, it just seems like an excuse to me. I'm positive I'm just not his type. I'm sure he doesn't like clingy and needy people. I can understand that.

But what hurts is that I really thought we had a connection. He was so easy to talk to and joke with. I felt comfortable with him. I haven't felt

comfortable around any man, except my brother and Matt, since…
everything happened back in the UK.

It's unusual for me to want to open up to anyone. Especially a
man. But I really did want to let down my walls for him. Feeling like that
scared me to death, but I grasped the feeling and dove head first into it. I
may have been through a lot of shit, but even I know that the past can't
define a person's entire life. I want to move past it.

I'm like any other woman. Well, most of them, anyway. I want to
settle down with a man who respects me. Someone who will be my partner
in life. Someone who is the other half of my heart and completes my soul.

I'd intended to take things slow and see how they flourished with
him. He seemed like he liked me and wanted to make a go of whatever
spark we felt in that hallway. I really thought he did anyway.

I guess I was the only person who felt it, though. Because it's me
who feels like she's dying. I'm the one who doesn't feel good enough to
hold the attention of a man like him. I'm sure he's out right now with
someone and probably doesn't remember my name. While I want to forget
any of this ever happened, I know I can't. It's just not who I am.

I barely acknowledge when Matt lifts me in his arms and opens the
door for Mariah. I keep clinging to him like a child. I probably wouldn't
even know Mariah is here had she not given me a light kiss on my
forehead and whispered in my ear that I'll be okay.

I feel so stupid for feeling like this over a guy I barely spoke to. It
seems so crazy to me. It's not lost on me that I'm acting like a teenager
who found out her celebrity crush got married. I know how ridiculous it is
to feel so hollow over a five-minute conversation with a man that I knew
the very moment I laid eyes on him I had no chance with. What's wrong
with me? Am I that fucked up?

I burrow into both Matt and Mariah when they crawl into my bed
with me. I don't have the strength to tell them they don't have to. And,
honestly, I really don't want them to leave. I know I won't be sleeping…

…but at least I won't be alone.

Chapter Six

☆ *DJ* ☆

I grin as I pull the young and ridiculously shy blonde woman sitting in my car into my arms. I slowly push her against the back door of my car as I close the passenger side I just tugged her from. She smiles up at me and wraps her arms around my waist with a sexy, needy whimper that makes my dick strain against the fabric of my pants.

She licks her lips as I lean down. My lips meet hers. My tongue teases her mouth until she opens it for me. She moans when I dive in and suck on her tongue. I let my hands fall to her ass and make their way under her barely there skirt. She giggles and wraps her arms around my shoulders and legs around my waist when I lift her.

Good. More of this. More to forget those pretty hazel eyes. Those sexy, pouty lips.

I growl and squeeze my eyes shut as I kiss down to her neck and nip. "I should probably get you inside," I drunkenly slur. "Before I end up giving my neighbors a show." I suck on her neck as I pull us both away from my car.

"Mmm… Such a wise police Captain."

I grin and squeeze her ass. Fleetingly, another pretty ass clouds my mind. An ass I'd love to bite. I push the thought away as quickly as it came to me. It's for the best. This is what I need.

I slightly stumble on the way to my front door. But I stay upright and keep nibbling on her neck. I make my way to her throat. I hum low and relish in her shiver. I kiss my way to the other side of her neck and continue sucking and nibbling.

"Okay, I can't fucking take this anymore," a deep male voice with a familiar accent growls.

I stop short, nearly dropping tonight's conquest. "The fuck?"

The girl squeaks and clings to me like she's terrified. "Who are you?"

"The man who is going to save you from a very embarrassing cab ride home after he fucks you and sends you packing. Let's just get you in a cab now, shall we?" Luca takes out his phone. I assume he's ordering an Uber because he never actually talks to anyone. "What's your address, sweetheart? Or shall I just put in the address of the University?"

"Oh my God!" she shrieks at him as I slowly let her down. "Who the hell do you think you are?"

Luca levels her with a glare that sends chills down my spine. She steps back and grips my arm. "The University it is." He types in an address and puts his phone away.

She looks up at me with a pout. "Are you going to let him talk to us like this? Who is he?"

I open my mouth to speak as I watch Luca, but no words come out. I don't know if it's because I'm so fucking wasted, or if it's because I'm surprised as hell he's standing in front of me at this time of night. It's after midnight. I know he has a job he starts tomorrow. He should be sleeping.

After I regain at least some semblance of my composure, I furrow my eyebrows in confusion. "Why are you here? What's going on?" My mind is pretty hazy from the numerous beers I drank, but I'm starting to think maybe something serious happened. "Are you okay?"

"You really want to discuss that in front of tonight's barely more than eighteen-year-old conquest?" His glare hasn't calmed in the slightest. In fact, it may have gotten harder.

I look down at the girl. I don't remember her name. It's not unusual. Remembering names of the women I pick to take home with me isn't a habit I tend to make. "I'm sorry. Really. I don't have a fuck of a clue why he's here, but whatever the reason, I don't want you to be a part of it." I turn when I hear a car pull up at the curb. "That was fucking quick."

"Yeah. Uber is a wonderful thing in a college town. Good thing this one was right around the corner," Luca glowers.

I glance at him as I lead my pouting conquest to the car. My dick disagrees with my decision to listen to Luca and send her away. As the car takes off, I reach down and adjust myself with a low growl. I turn back to Luca, who is leaning against the side of my house with his arms folded over his chest. He's still glaring at me, which does nothing more than piss me off.

"What the fuck is wrong with you?" I ask when I reach him. I'm already feeling the effects of what is going to be a hangover to rival all of the hangovers I've had over the course of my life. "Why are you here?"

He raises an eyebrow before he stands to his full height. I don't have a chance to dodge the right hook he throws before it meets my jaw, but I do catch myself before I hit the ground. It doesn't make a difference, though, because his left fist connects with my stomach. I double over. I try to catch my breath, but Luca throws an uppercut that knocks me on my ass.

"Holy fuck," I pant as I cough and roll slowly to my side. I hold my stomach. "Fuck me," I moan. I close my eyes and roll back onto my back.

All of my police training is forgotten. Usually, I'd be doing all I can to fight. Get back up. But all I can think of right now is the pain coursing through my body as I try to keep all of the alcohol in my system from ending up all over me. When I'm convinced enough that I'm not going to start puking, I dare to open my eyes.

Luca is standing over me. He's got that same fierce as hell glare plastered all over his face as he looks down at me. He could do a lot of damage right now, and I probably wouldn't be able to do a fucking thing about it. The thought strikes a little fear into me, but not as much as the idea that I'm going to throw up.

I quickly turn to my side as the alcohol sloshing around in my jolted stomach makes its way at a very rapid pace up my throat and into my mouth. I barely get to my hands and knees before it comes out.

I watch Luca out of the corner of my eye while I lose the contents of my stomach. He doesn't move an inch. The alcohol burned going down, but it feels like fucking lava coming back up. I'm pretty positive it left scorch marks on my throat and burned the lining of my stomach to cinders.

"Fuck," I whimper when I finally finish. I carefully sit back on my heels and wipe my mouth with the back of my hand.

"Serves you right."

I look up at Luca with a cold glare of my own. "Why the fuck are you here?"

He reaches out a hand for me to take so he can help me up. I glare at it for a few moments before I finally get up on my own. If he weren't a friend, I'd probably kick his ass. Lucky for him, I don't even know where the hell I am right now.

I scrub my hands down my face.

House.

My house.

I hear him sigh as I turn and walk to my door. I unlock it and walk into my house, leaving it open for him. I don't turn around or look at him. I head for my kitchen and listen as he closes the door behind him. I grab a bottle of water for both of us out of my refrigerator. I set his on the counter and open mine.

Luca follows me cautiously into the kitchen and doesn't take his eyes off me as he opens the bottle. He takes a drink while the two of us glare at each other. The punches he landed and the puking have done wonders to clear my mind.

Whatever is happening has to do with Lyric. The damn girl I was doing pretty fucking well at forgetting.

"You might want to clean up. I split your lip and probably gave you a black eye."

I run my thumb across my lip with a shrug. I can already feel the dried blood. Judging from the pain in my cheek, I'm fairly certain the eye is swollen. I might regret it tomorrow, but I'll be damned if I do something to make myself look weak in front of this kid.

Fuck all of that.

"Not a chance in hell." I take a long drink of my water as I head for my couch and sit down.

Luca sighs and shakes his head. He opens the freezer and finds an ice pack. After he grabs his bottle of water, he walks to my couch and sits next to me. He doesn't give me a choice. He just puts the ice pack against my eye and holds it there.

"We left the UK because I fucked a guy up after he beat up Lyric," he says before I have a chance to remove his hand and the ice pack from my face. Or land a punch of my own.

I slowly turn to look at him. "What?" I swallow hard. My heart actually feels a little like it broke. I rub my chest with one hand and take over holding the ice pack with the other.

Luca sits back and stares at the sliding glass door leading to my patio. He takes a drink of his water before he continues. "Lyric was bullied most of her life. My parents. Kids at school. Kids in our high school. She was pushed. Shoved. Spat on. She was hit. She was kicked when she fell after being shoved. I can't tell you the number of times I came across her in the halls crying on the floor as she was picking up her books or papers."

"Shit." I feel a little like he sucker punched me once again with those words.

"You think that's bad? It's nowhere near the worst." He takes a long drink of his water as I watch him. After a long silence, he takes a breath. "When we graduated, we both thought it was over. We moved out as soon as we were allowed. We got jobs. We were doing well. She started dating this guy. I didn't really like him all that much, but I'd never stop her from dating someone she liked. I thought the guy was a dick. To her, though, he was always an angel. At least in front of me."

"Why do I get the feeling this is going to take an ugly turn?" I ask quietly as I turn my gaze outside.

I have no right to feel like I want to rip this dude's head off. I don't know him. I don't even know what happened. I certainly have no claim to Lyric, so wanting to kill whoever Luca is talking about is crazy.

Luca chuckles. "Your feeling is correct. She called me one night. I almost didn't answer. My phone was on silent. I was on a date. We were in the middle of…" He glances at me.

"I get it."

He nods. "I just got the feeling something was wrong. I paused right before the entrance point and sat up. I was kind of startled. My chest felt tight all of the sudden. I grabbed my phone. I didn't know she was calling because my phone was silenced. I answered. She was screaming and crying. I barely got it out of her, but she said he'd slapped her. She ran because she was scared. He was yelling after her. I was surprised as fuck that she ran. That's not like her. She would usually be frozen in fear at that point." He pauses to take a drink. "I obviously left. I went to her. She shut down, DJ. Completely. She didn't say a single word to me or anyone for an entire week."

"Shit," I whisper a second time. I already know where this is going.

"When she finally did, she blamed herself for everything. The yelling. The argument. The slap. She felt like she was the cause of it. She said he got pissed at her because she wanted to cuddle with him, but she'd been doing it all day and most of the day before. He pushed her away and said he needed space. He got mad when she started tearing up. She immediately felt that she was in the wrong. She was too needy and clingy to him. She tried to make it up to him the only way she knew how." His face turns up in a scowl. "She figured making him physically happy and satisfied would make him forgive her for making him angry. She doesn't believe she's good with words, even though she is. She feels like she can express herself better through actions."

I take another long drink and toss the ice pack on the table. I take a breath after I finish the bottle. "I take it that didn't work."

He shrugs. "It did for a few minutes. At least until after he got off. Then the real fight began. It took her a long time to get over that. She still has scars from it. Emotional, I mean." He leans forward and puts his empty bottle on the table. After another few silent moments, he takes another breath. "I'm going to need something a lot stronger for the rest of this."

I nod. "Say no more." I stand and find a bottle of beer in the fridge. Knowing I've more than surpassed my limit, and feeling like I need to be sober for this, I grab another bottle of water for myself. I hand him the beer and put another on the table for him as I sit back down.

Luca takes a long gulp of the dark brew. After a few minutes, he leans back once more and puts his feet on the table. "It took her almost six years to date again. And the guy she started dating was one of my friends. A close one. Someone I considered family."

I watch him a few moments before opening my bottle. My throat is suddenly very dry. My stomach is tied into a tighter knot than a Navy sailor can dream of making. "Fuck."

Luca chuckles before downing the bottle and opening the other one. "He'd spent about a year wooing her. He was really good with her. I mean, he really charmed her. He was friends with her first. He proved to her that not all men are assholes. When they started dating, I don't think I'd ever seen her as happy as she was. I swear to fuck, I thought he was going to marry her. She was talking about moving in with him. I was making plans to move my girlfriend into our apartment. One night, I came home from work. She was really upset. She was crying. She said she thought she'd messed up with him by going back to her old ways. I guess she'd had a panic attack over not being able to find her keys or something. When it was over, she was kind of clinging to him. She said she was needy. She'd made him late to work. He got upset with her and left angry." He takes a sip. I'm glad he's slowing down with this one.

I take a sip of my water. It's amazing how quickly one becomes sober when circumstances require it. I scrub a hand down my face because it's better than ripping the couch cushion underneath me apart. I rub my chest.

I don't want to ask what I'm about to, but I do. "Did he hit her, too?"

He takes another sip and shakes his head slowly. "Not then."

I let my head fall back on the couch as I close my eyes. "Fuck."

I feel like I'm having a heart attack. I'm torn between being the fucking wall she needs to keep her safe from every asshole that tries to fuck with her and killing every single person who has ever hurt her.

"Over the next couple of years, Lyric started to change. She got quiet. She'd jump at the smallest noise. Like, if I was putting a plate away and it clanged against another plate, she'd jolt. She'd get lost in thought. She actually started forgetting things. Lyric had never done that before. She'd write things down but forget she'd written it down. She'd take Tylenol for a headache but forget she took them and take more. She had anxiety and panic disorder from an early age because of the bullying, but as she got older, we'd worked on it. She was doing well. And my friend had been doing well with her, too. So, her change in behavior set me on edge. But she absolutely wouldn't open up to me about it. She kept saying it was okay."

"But it wasn't."

"Nope." He pops the 'p' in the single word and takes another sip. "I came home the night Lyric said she would be starting to move out. I had my girlfriend with me. It was pretty quiet. I thought she'd already left. I started messing around with my girl, but she stopped me. She said she thought she heard a muffled scream. Before those words fully left her mouth, I took off for the stairs. Twin ESP or something. I ran directly to her room. My girlfriend was on my heels and somehow passed me on the stairs. She busted into Lyric's room like a fucking warrior princess. She stopped short and screamed so loud, I'm positive she woke the dead."

I pinch the bridge of my nose. "The things I'm thinking -"

"Aren't anywhere near what we walked in on." He takes a long drink before he continues. "Lyric had a private bathroom. I guess I just felt like that was fair when we got our place together. I wanted her to feel both safe and comfortable, but also that she had privacy. You know?"

"Yeah. Yeah, I get it."

"She was bent over the bathtub. She was naked. Struggling. He was fully clothed, but we could tell he was fucking her from behind. His fingers were tangled in her hair. He was holding her down in the water of the bathtub. The shower head was running water over her. He'd let her up long enough for her to cough and sputter. As soon as she started screaming at him to stop, though, he pushed her back down." Luca's voice cracks.

I look over at him just as he swipes the back of his hand over his eyes. "Holy fuck." I feel like my chest is going to collapse. "I don't even know what to say."

"I ripped him off of her. I slammed him against the wall while my girlfriend helped Lyric. Lyric was flailing and fighting when she came up. Screaming. But I barely heard her. I was too busy beating her boyfriend to within an inch of his life."

"I don't blame you," I say quietly. I pat his arm.

"You keep asking me why we left the UK. Well, that's why. I made him a deal. He stayed the fuck away from my sister, and I let him live. A couple of days later, I called him. He said he had no intention of pressing charges, but he wanted me to stay away from him. I told him he didn't need to worry about me as long as he stayed away from her. He said he knew Lyric wanted to move to the United States. He knew it was a lifelong dream of hers to be here. We made an agreement. I moved with her to the US. He kept his mouth shut. I decided it was a good deal because even if we had managed to get him charged with rape and attempted murder, he probably would have ended up pleading out and been out of jail in a couple of years."

"And you would have ended up in jail for assault."

"Probably aggravated assault or attempted murder. His injuries were pretty severe. He spent the night in the hospital and almost a year at his parents' house after that. I wasn't kidding when I said I fucked him up. I probably would have killed him. My girlfriend tried to pull me back, but it didn't work. The only thing that worked was Lyric on her knees in front of me. She was protecting him. Begging me to stop. She was bleeding from places she shouldn't have been." He takes a breath. "He'd torn her ass apart. She was bruised all over. Including…" He trails off and shakes his head. He doesn't need to tell me where. I swallow down the fury bubbling up. "He was unconscious by that time. To this day, I don't know how he got to the hospital, and how I didn't end up in cuffs."

I sit forward and rest my hands on my knees. "So, you left to avoid charges."

"I left to protect my sister. I didn't give a fuck if I ended up in prison. I can take it. But if that had happened, Lyric would have had no one. He could have done whatever he wanted to her. And he probably would have. I don't regret my actions. If I could have changed anything about what I did, I wouldn't have. But if I had killed him, I would have gone to jail. Lyric wouldn't have been able to handle that. She would have blamed herself for my actions. I broke my hand during the beating. She blamed herself for the pain I was in. She put her own emotions aside to take care of me."

"Maybe she was trying to find a way to cope. Taking care of you was her way of doing that."

Luca leans forward and puts his empty bottle on the table. "She spent the full three months it took us to get our six month visitor's passports approved blaming herself for what happened."

I look at him. "What? Why?"

He shrugs. "Because it's who she is." He rests his elbows on his knees and meets my eyes. "He spent the entire time they were together preying on all of her vulnerabilities, DJ. She's submissive. Not just submissive, but a natural submissive. It's just who she is. She does better following orders. Uh..." He looks outside again. "People told her all the time that she wasn't good enough. She wasn't pretty enough. She was too fat. Or too skinny. She's been told she's stupid. And she believes it all when things happen. Like when he was trying to kill her. She believed it was her fault. She was too clingy. She didn't remember something he told her. Every time he..." He takes another breath. "Every time he hit her, yelled at her, or..." He trails off and shakes his head. "Or forced her to do things she didn't want to, she took it as a punishment."

"Jesus... Christ."

"Remember when I said she started having memory issues?"

"Yeah?"

He nods slowly but keeps his eyes forward. "It was because of him. He'd slap her, but he'd slap her on the head. So he didn't leave bruises. At least where I could see them. The entire time they were together, he was abusing her. He'd tell her she was fat. So, she stopped eating. He'd tell her she was stupid if she couldn't explain something. So, she started believing she was stupid and wasn't good with words. She believed her worth lay completely in her actions. Sexual. How happy she could make him. She got quiet because every time she opened her mouth, he would find something about what she said to be unintelligent. Her sense of humor became non-existent because he told her she wasn't funny. After it was all over, Lyric had dropped close to a hundred pounds. She started having constant nightmares. Constant. If I wasn't sleeping next to her, she couldn't sleep. She'd be awake for days because she was terrified of the dreams she'd have if she fell asleep. She'd finally just collapse, but she'd wake up after only a few hours because of the nightmares. I barely got her to eat more than crackers and broth."

I say nothing. Not because I don't know what to say, but because I know if I say anything it's going to be something about asking him where the fuckers who hurt her are. Every single one of them. Including the parents.

I say nothing because I don't have the right to. Lyric is not only not mine, but she deserves the fucking world. More than what I can give her. More than the asshole I am. She needs someone who can take care of her. Show her that she's a fucking Queen that the entire universe should and does revolve around.

I suck in a sharp breath when it all hits me. The reason Luca showed up on my doorstep and laid me out. I can feel my hands start to shake. My hands never fucking shake. I'm the steadiest person I know.

"Fucking hell." I stand and walk unsteadily towards my patio doors. But I don't walk out of the room. I turn to Luca. As I knew he would be, he's watching me. Waiting for me to realize everything that I just did.

I'm sick to my stomach.

Horrified.

"Do you understand the reason I'm here now?" he asks me quietly after a long stare down.

"She thinks my text message means she's not good enough for me."

"She thinks you meant that you don't want her. That she's not good enough. She thinks she was too clingy and needy. Too..." He pauses, obviously searching for the right words.

"Too pushy. Because she texted me a few times, and I didn't respond. Not until I sent her the text that told her I didn't want to ruin our friendship, and that I wasn't relationship material."

He nods and stands slowly. "Yeah. All of that. And it took her back to her past. She put the blame squarely on herself. She decided that she's not your type. That's why you didn't want her. She's not pretty enough. Not like the girls you take to bed. She's not confident enough. Flirty enough. She thinks she's both unwantable, unfuckable, and completely stupid for thinking that she had a shot with a guy who is out of her league. I left her sobbing in Matt's arms to come here. She doesn't blame you at all. And she fucking should." He pauses and takes another breath. "You know what she said to me before I left? She begged me not to hurt you. Because it was her fault."

I shake my head and lean against the glass door. "I need to fucking fix this." I say the words to myself, but Luca hears them.

"Yeah. You do." He takes his beer bottles and my water bottles to the kitchen and puts them in my recycle bin. "I don't know why I'm even considering giving you a second chance with her. I'm tired of her being hurt. I think it's because, this time, I think you both need each other. I don't think I'll be able to bring her back this time. I think, this time, you're the only one who can do it. And if you don't, well, I guess I'll be kissing my citizenship goodbye."

I can't help but chuckle at that. "Why? Because you'll end up pummeling me?"

He looks at me so seriously that the small smile on my lips drops instantaneously. "No. Because I won't be able to watch her spiral this time. My heart can't handle it. Lyric doesn't deserve that. I'd do whatever I have to do to make her happy again. And that includes taking her away from all of this. Whether that be in the physical or spiritual world…" He shrugs and trails off.

My heart stops beating. I swallow hard. "You don't mean you think this would drive her to kill herself."

"She's had thoughts before." He puts his hands up as if he's trying to ward off what he thinks I'm about to say. "I'm not trying to guilt you, DJ. I'm not. That's not my intention. I'm being upfront and honest with you. She's barely holding on after what happened to her in the UK. This, in retrospect to that, is small. And most people would be upset for a while then move on. But not her. It's just the kind of thing to finally push her over the edge." He puts his hands on the counter. "So, I'm asking you. Either fix it, or stay away from her so I can, at the very least, try."

He watches me a few moments before he takes a deep breath. He walks slowly towards the door. In the period of time I've known Luca, I've never seen him look so defeated. Sad, even. Dejected. I don't like seeing my friend upset.

It pales in comparison to the pain I'm feeling at hurting Lyric, though. I thought I was protecting her from being hurt. I didn't realize I was shattering her. I hate the idea of everything she went through. It makes me sick to know the people she thought she could trust broke her in so many ways.

I feel like throwing up. It's not until I hear the front door close that I spring into action. It's time for me to grow up. The fact that it took this to make me realize it is not something I'm proud of, but I'll take what I can get.

I quickly catch up to Luca just as he's ducking into his car. "Luca. Wait."

He looks up at me, exhausted. "Yeah?"

"You okay to drive?" I ask in concern.

"Yeah. I'm not drunk. Or buzzed. I'm just fucking tired. I'm tired of this happening to her." He slides into the car.

I lean a hand on his door and the roof of his car. "This is a long shot, but you think you can wait a minute? Let me grab an overnight bag. I'll sleep on the couch, but I want to talk to Lyric. I don't want to put it off."

He watches me for a moment. Finally, he nods. "Just... make this right, DJ. For both of you. She deserves more." He gets the rest of the way into his car before looking back up at me. "So do you. I just... I want you both to be happy. Mostly her. I don't want her hurting anymore. And I do trust you. As crazy as it seems, considering what Lyric and I have been through with my friends."

"I'm not like that, Luca. I'd never do anything like that."

"I know. Hurry up. I've been away from her for too long. Matt and Mariah are with her, but..."

I nod, fully understanding. "I won't be long."

I hurry back into the house and throw things into a gym bag. For the first time in my life, I'm listening to my heart. I've always been the type of man who does what makes sense. All of my marriages only happened because it seemed like the logical step after being with them for the length of time I was. The divorces happened because it was the right thing to do. My whole life has been led with my head.

But not this time. This time, I'm letting my heart take the lead. My heart is telling me that Lyric deserves more. She deserves me to be a better man not only for her, but for myself. She needs me to make this right. She needs to understand that she's an amazing woman.

Because contrary to how I felt earlier today, the woman holds my heart in her hand. And she deserves to know that she's the only one to ever have that power over me.

Chapter Seven

☆ Lyric ☆

Bacon.

I sniff as I sleepily open my eyes. Luca must be making bacon. He knows I'll be upset today. He's trying to circumvent it by bribing me with one of my favorite foods. I glance at the clock on my dresser and sigh. He'll have to leave soon. He has a new construction job, but he promised me that he'll still be able to do all he needs to for the police ball.

I bite my lip thinking of the police ball. I'd been so excited for it because it's the biggest event that I've ever had the opportunity to plan. It's so important to the department. But that happiness and giddiness I'd been feeling is gone. Because each time I think of police, I think of DJ.

I'm not even sure it's even a good idea for me to continue with this. Maybe with me there, the other officers won't have as much fun. I'm sure DJ wouldn't want to see me. I sniffle and slowly walk to the bathroom to wash my face.

I chew the inside of my cheek when I see how puffy my eyes are. I must have cried myself to sleep. The last thing I remember is Mariah and Matt telling me that it's not my fault. I vaguely remember Luca taking their spot sometime during the night and hugging me until I dozed back off.

I want to believe them, but it's not easy. I know it's my fault. Everything about this is my fault. I'm the one who allowed myself to feel hurt over a person who never made any promises to me. He hardly even talked to me. I'm the one who was stupid enough to believe I had a shot with him. Then I ruined it by bothering him. It is all my fault. No matter what they say.

I wipe my face when I'm done washing it. I can feel tears burn my eyes, but I think I'm incapable of crying anymore. I feel dry. I sniffle anyway. I wish I were different. I wish I didn't push people away. Repulse them. Like I did to…

I turn away from the mirror. Like I did to my ex. If I hadn't made him so upset, I wouldn't have ended up being punished… with the water from the shower over my head. With the water in the bathtub. I dig my nails into my arm as I hug myself and walk slowly to the kitchen. I try not to think about it, but I can't stop myself. I made him angry. I rightfully got punished.

"Lyric?"

I shake my head to rid the images I've managed to conjure up. I smile softly and open my mouth to speak, but immediately close it when I see DJ standing right in front of me. I whimper and take a step back with wide eyes. My nails dig deeper into my arm because I'm trying to wake myself up.

I trip over myself and fall backwards. How I manage to end up in a chair is something I'll have to revisit later. Right now, DJ's strong, fresh, masculine, earthy scent is overpowering all of me. I don't know what's happening, but he's here.

I watch him with wolf cub eyes as he kneels in front of me. "Lyric."

"What?" I squeak, still hugging myself. I don't even feel the nails in my arms anymore.

He slowly takes my wrists. He doesn't take his eyes off mine. I'm trembling. I know I am, but I'm powerless to stop it. It's not even because I'm scared. I don't feel any fear towards DJ. It's a strange thing. Each of my past relationships set off numerous alarm bells in my head right from the very beginning. Thinking back on them now, I can name all of them.

But not with DJ. DJ's warm, large hands wrapped around my wrists is comforting. His deep voice rumbling when he says my name is soothing. His striking green eyes set me at ease. When he lowers my hands to my thighs and rubs his thumbs over the sensitive flesh on the underside of my wrists, I nearly melt.

His smile warms me from the inside. "You okay?" he asks me softly.

"Uh…" My mind races with everything I want to say, but I know I have no chance of getting any of it out. I can't even decipher anything right now.

"I know I fucked up. And I want to talk about it, but Luca forced me to take an oath in blood that I would feed you first. So, I made bacon and waffles."

Despite my nerves, my stomach growls. I shakily lick my lips. "W-with chocolate syrup?" I whisper.

He gives me a half smile that sets me on fire. "And strawberries."

I slowly nod and let him pull me up from the chair. He takes my hand in his and gently tugs me to the kitchen with him. When we reach the stools, I start to let go of his hand to sit down. Instead, DJ keeps my hand in his. I look up at him in surprise and confusion, but say nothing.

He takes a plate and sets it in front of me. He puts a waffle on the plate with some bacon. I watch him spread butter over it with a butter knife. He holds the plate with the hand holding mine so it doesn't move, but he doesn't let go of me. He pours chocolate syrup over it. I watch him as he puts some whipped cream in the middle.

I chew the inside of my lip while I watch him prepare his own with butter and maple syrup. When he finishes, he takes fresh strawberries he's already cut up and puts them on top of both of our waffles. I'd never tell him, but I'm grateful to him for not letting go of my hand. I think it might be the only thing keeping me upright. I don't understand it.

I reach for my plate when he reaches for his, but he surprises me and takes them both. I look up at him and try to pull my hand away again so he doesn't drop them, but he holds it tighter and nudges me towards our small table on the other side of the counter. He carries the plates with an ease that makes me wonder if he'd been a server or something.

But I don't ask. I don't want to upset him by opening my mouth.

He puts both plates on the table and pulls out a chair. He helps me sit and pulls his own chair closer. When he sits, he rests his thigh against mine. The contact is beyond soothing, but I don't know why. He slowly lets go of my hand as he quietly digs into his waffle. I watch him for a few moments, unsure what exactly it is he's trying to accomplish, before slowly starting to eat.

The waffle is amazing, and I close my eyes to enjoy the taste even more. It tastes a little like there's vanilla in it. It's light and everything a waffle should be. The bacon is crisp and perfect. The slices are thick. Paired with the waffle, I'm in tastebud heaven.

I take quick glances around the room while I eat small bites. I don't like eating in front of anyone. I've always been told I eat too much. Or too fast. Or I take too big of bites. Now, I make sure I eat slowly. I cut my waffle with a knife and fork. My bites are far smaller than DJ's.

To keep my mind from slipping back to everyone who has ever insulted me, I focus on our apartment. It's an open floor plan. There's a giant floor to ceiling window that spans the entire living room. It looks out over a duck pond on the property of the apartment complex Luca and I live in. There's a glass door off the left side of the living room that leads out to a small, private balcony. There's a black mesh screen over the open part of the balcony to keep bugs out. It also keeps the balcony fairly cool, even when it's ninety degrees and humid.

We have a dark-brown, L-shaped couch on the right side of the living room. The TV is Luca's pride and joy. It's a large, sixty-five-inch Samsung Smart TV that's mounted to the wall on the left side of the room.

Off the left side of the living room is Luca's bedroom. The kitchen is off the living room. It's rather large, considering the apartment itself isn't that big. There's a small space between the kitchen and living room where we have the table sitting against the wall. There's a small bathroom near it.

Off the right side of the living room is my bedroom. It's attached to a private bathroom. There's also a small closet that hides our washer and dryer. Next to it is another small closet where we put our shoes.

I feel DJ's hand on my upper thigh. I jump as my eyes dart to his. He gives me a soft smile but keeps his hand where it is. It's not lost on me that his leg is still against mine. He hasn't lost contact with me ever since he gripped my wrists. He'll never know just how much the contact is helping me.

"I asked you if you were full," he says softly.

"S-sorry." I look down at my plate as I chew nervously on my bottom lip. There's still almost a whole piece of bacon left and a quarter of the waffle. I nod, but the truth is, I'm not full. I'm still hungry. But there's only one person in this entire world who wouldn't judge me if I finished my plate and asked for more.

Luca.

DJ looks at me suspiciously. I instantly regret lying to him, but I've learned my lesson. I've learned it well. No one wants to see a woman eat everything on her plate. They'll call her fat. A pig. Look down at her.

So, while I do want to finish the delectable food DJ obviously worked hard to make, I won't. I already disappointed him and made him regret giving me his phone number. I don't know why he's here, but I won't make him look even more down on me than he already does. I'm sure the women he's used to eat nothing but lettuce. And they probably don't even finish that.

"Lyric," DJ says softly, but commandingly. I can't help but look up at him, though I say nothing. "Finish eating."

My eyes widen. I swallow hard as I shake my head. "I'm full. Really."

"Except I know you aren't. Your stomach is still growling, and you keep looking at it like you want to finish it, but you don't think you should. I had a very long conversation with Luca last night, honey. I know a lot of the things you went through. One of them being with food. So, please. Finish. And know that I'm not going to sit here and call you fat. You're far from it." He runs his thumb over my lower lip and tugs it a little. "Stop biting your lip."

"I'm sorry, sir," I whisper as I release it.

"Don't apologize. Just don't do it." He stands slowly and kisses the top of my head. "Finish your breakfast, please."

It's the first time he's broken contact. I instantly miss him, but I obey and finish my food while he starts washing the dishes. By the time I finish, he's nearly done with the dishes and everything involved with cleaning up. I get up and walk to the kitchen. I stand hesitantly a few feet away from him with my plate. He looks over his shoulder at me with a smile.

"Um... I'm done." I say the words quietly and show him my plate, feeling slightly foolish. Does he think this makes me look like a child?

64

Will he hate that I really want the praise from him after obeying his command?

He smiles. "Good girl. Come here." His voice rumbles as he gestures me to his side with a flick of his head.

I sidle next to him, careful not to touch him without his permission, but quietly relishing in his praise. I don't want to come off needy, but all I want is contact. It's something that bothered my exes. Me constantly needing to feel them in some way was an annoyance. I don't want him to think that about me. I know he already does.

DJ takes my plate with one hand and a handful of soap suds in the other. Before I can react to what he's doing, the suds are on my nose and my head. I'd squeak or squawk, but I'm so surprised that no sound comes out, even though my mouth is hanging open in shock.

DJ laughs and puts my plate in the dish water. I walk around him and grab a towel to dry off. I smile a little. When he finishes the dishes, he gently takes the towel I'd just used and drops it over the clean dishes. He holds out his hand.

I hesitate, but take it. He leads me to the couch and sits. He, once again, doesn't let go of my hand. I watch him put his long legs up on the lounge part of the couch. His blue jeans are loose fitting, but he's so muscular that I don't think anything would be truly loose on him. His dark red t-shirt strains across his chest. I'm sure the shirt would be big on anyone else, but not him.

When he's comfortable, he starts to pull me in his lap, but I attempt to sit next to him instead. I should have known he wouldn't let me do that. He lets go of my hand and grips my waist instead. He pulls me into his lap so my side is flush against his chest.

I know I'm blushing as I look down. "DJ... I... don't understand what's happening. I thought... you -"

"Would you be upset with me if I asked you to let me talk first?"

"No, sir," I close my mouth, but don't look up. "I'm sorry."

He tangles one of his hands in my hair and tugs just enough so I'm looking at him. When Matt did that, it was a command to look at him. But when DJ does it, it seems almost like a plea and command. Something far more intimate. His other hand drops to my thigh and hip. He pulls me close.

"Lyric, listen to me. I fucked up. I did. I gave you my number because you blew me away. I've never been dumbstruck by anyone before. I knew as soon as you said your name who you were. Your brother has been trying to set me up with you for a while, but I've been avoiding it. That has nothing to do with you. It has to do with me. I've been married three times. Divorced three times. After the last one, I just decided I wasn't relationship material. I figured if I wanted sex one night, I'd find a girl willing to give it up. There are plenty of them in this city. A lot who have no problem having a one-night stand with a cop."

I continue to avoid his gaze and try to stay as still as possible. I don't want to make a wrong move, but I know he's trying to let me down easily right now. "I understand." My voice is barely a whisper.

"No. I don't think you do, sweet girl."

I take a breath and nod. "It's okay, DJ. I know I'm not -"

"Lyric. That isn't what I'm saying, honey. Shut your mind off. Look at me." He makes no move to make me look at him this time. He keeps one hand tangled in my hair and the other on my hip. He expects me to obey.

So, I do.

I slowly turn to look at him. I'm sure I'll see exactly what I fear in his eyes. I'm sure I'll see that he doesn't want me. That I'm not like the girls he does want and like. It's a thought I have ingrained in me. I've never been good enough.

But what I see is exactly the opposite. I see something I've never seen in anyone other than Luca, Matt, and Mariah. Understanding. Acceptance. I tilt my head a little because there's something else. I can't place it, but it makes his eyes sparkle.

"You aren't like the women I've been with. What you don't understand, though, is that it isn't a bad thing. It's what makes you special. Different from all of them. It's what makes me want to talk to you. Spend time with you. Get to know you. It's what made me give you my number in the first place. And it's what scares the hell out of me. All of that. I've never had an instant connection to anyone like I did with you. That's the reason I sent you that text. Not because of anything you did. I wanted to text you back. Hell. I wanted to take you on a date and do all of that stuff that I haven't done in a long time. And for the first time in my life, I wanted to do it because I genuinely like you. Not because it's what I thought was expected of me."

I stay quiet as I listen to him. After a few moments, I reach up and rub my chest. I'm having a lot of trouble keeping up. So many thoughts are running through my head. I can't decipher them. I keep thinking of my past and how my exes reacted to me. How they pushed me away and said I was clingy.

But everything DJ is doing is exactly the opposite of them. Instead of putting distance between us, he's maintained almost constant contact. It's like he knows touch is reassuring to me. I don't know if it's because Luca told him, or if he just senses it.

I take a deep breath. "I don't…" I trail off and lower my eyes. I don't know what to say or do right now. I feel lost. I'm trying to keep my hands clasped together in my lap, but I need to grip something. So, I drop them between my legs and grip my thighs.

"Last night, Luca paid me a visit. He told me…" DJ takes a breath and grips my hip and thigh a little harder. I look down. I expect him to push me away now. There's no way he could want me after knowing about my past.

Instead, he drops his hand from my hair and wraps his arms around me. It's like he's cradling me in his lap. I turn my face into his neck and shift just enough to press as close as I can to him. It feels like the most normal thing in the world with him. It doesn't feel like it did with my exes. He doesn't stiffen. He doesn't push me away. He pulls me closer.

I tremble against him and close my eyes. I give in and grip his shirt. It's impossible to fight the natural urge to do it. It's better than trying to talk. I don't know what to say. I can't make sense of what's happening. I can't keep up with my racing mind.

After a few long moments of DJ just holding me, he finally speaks. I'm surprised to feel a slight dampness in my hair.

DJ is crying.

"He told me what happened to you in the UK. All of it. From the bullying. Your parents. People in school. He told me about your exes and what happened with them. He told me… the… reason you left."

I squeeze my eyes closed. "I'm sorry…"

"Lyric. My God, little girl, it's not your fault." I feel his lips against the top of my head. "It's not your fault. It's not your fault that I freaked out and sent you a text that made you feel like you weren't good enough. You are good enough. You're so fucking far above my level, it's insane. You didn't deserve what happened to you then. And, fuck, you don't deserve what I did to you. What you deserve is the entire fucking world and more. You deserve everything good. Everything, Lyric. I don't deserve you. I'll understand if you tell me to leave, but I'm asking you for the second chance I don't fucking deserve. A second chance to prove to you that I'm worthy of you. Let me be that man who gave you his number. The one who had good intentions and wanted to spend time with you and get to know you. I promise I won't hurt you like that again."

I'm quiet for a long while. I grip DJ's shirt. His fingertips dig into my hip. With his other hand, he lightly rubs my arm. I chew on the inside of my cheek as I think. My thoughts are becoming a little clearer. They're at least here. In the present.

But there's one thing I can't get past. Something that I feel I need to ask him. "You know about my past," I finally say against his chest.

He jumps slightly. I'm sure because it's been silent for such a long period. "I do."

I sniffle. It's not something I want to ask. I'm not sure I even want the answer. But my heart hurts. I know I need to know. "Are you just… here… because you feel… sorry for me?" The words leave my mouth. I'm proud of myself for asking, but I don't feel any better. I know his answer will either break me completely or put me back together. At least a little.

"No," he says with no hesitation. "Fuck no, Lyric. I understand why you'd think that. I won't sit here and lie to you and say that I don't feel bad about what happened to you. And I won't tell you that I don't feel sorry for you. It's hard not to, honey. But that isn't why I'm here. I'm here because I realize that I fucked up with you. I let my own issues and beliefs about myself get in the way of potentially starting something real with an incredible woman. That's on me. That's my fault. My own stupidity. That has absolutely nothing to do with you. Nothing to do with what you went through. It has to do with what I went through."

I finally allow my eyes to open but don't move to look at him. "Help me understand. I want to. Why did you say you weren't relationship material?"

I feel him smile against the top of my head, but I can tell it's sad. Maybe his story is just as unhappy as mine.

Chapter Eight

☆ DJ ☆

I close my eyes and smile against the top of her head. I owe it to her. She deserves to know my story. It might help her understand the reasoning I had for trying to protect her from me. The reason I feel like she's so much better than I am and deserves so much more than me and what I can give her.

"I got married young. It didn't last long. She liked the idea of being a cop's wife. The wife of a guy in the military. She loved the idea of being with a dominant man. The allure wore off quickly. We were done within a couple of years. She didn't like that I'd be away for months at a time on deployments. She didn't like the hours I put in. She didn't like that I didn't wear a wedding band at work. Lots of cops don't. People look at rings as a weakness. While I wanted to wear it, I didn't. It was a way to protect her and myself out there. I didn't want people I dealt with seeing a wedding ring and deciding that to get to me, they could go through her. Some cops don't view it that way, but I deal with a lot of scum. I did a lot of undercover stuff during those earlier years. That was another reason. I didn't want to portray that I was a happily married man when I was trying to take down a drug dealer."

She nods slowly. "You wanted to protect her."

"It's in my nature to want to protect. It's who I am. But she took it as a sign I must be cheating. So, she did. After we split, I remarried a few years later. I had been with her for quite a while. It seemed like the next logical step in our relationship. Like what was expected of me. I guess I felt like after three years, she deserved a commitment. Her parents were ecstatic, but we both figured out pretty quickly that we didn't want to be married. At least not to each other. I found out later that she cheated on me with another guy. She ended up marrying him. They've been together for something like twelve years, though, so I guess it worked out for the best."

She nods slowly again while I run my fingers through her hair. "You wanted what was best for her."

I smile into her hair. "You have an uncanny ability to see the positive in situations that wrecked me. You're right. I was being protective. I did want the best for them and me. But it wasn't looked at like that by them. To them, I was controlling. Smothering. Uncaring. Unkind. After the second divorce, I decided fuck it. I'll just hit the bars and get my kicks when I need it. Other than that, I'd decided I was focusing on my job. I didn't need anything else. It was pretty obvious to me that I just wasn't marriage and relationship material, but I gave it another chance. Third time's a charm, right?"

She shrugs softly and shifts. "I guess I don't really know." She grips my shirt a little harder as she lowers her hand more towards my waistband.

Luca gave me a heads up before he left this morning on how Lyric will behave and what I need to do to make her more comfortable. I already knew most of it. I knew she felt like I'd rejected her and would need me to make her feel wanted. I figured out during my talk last night with him that Lyric gets comfort and reassurance with touch.

I guess I can see how some view that as needy, but I never could. It's not who I am. Making sure my girl has everything she needs is who I am. Pushing her away when all she needs is to feel loved is never something I'd ever be able to do. Above and beyond that, I don't understand why the hell a man wouldn't want a beautiful woman to touch him or gain comfort from him.

I take a chance and kiss her head gently. I'd never tell her that the move is more to steady my racing heart than it is for her. "Marriage three was sort of me telling the world to fuck off. I'd proven to myself up until that point that I wasn't cut out for marriage or relationships. I'd been in a couple of relationships that ended just as disastrously as my marriages. So, when my soon to be wife number three made it past the three-week mark dating me, I was slightly optimistic. But I absolutely put a halt on a lot of things. I toned down my dominant nature. I let her take the lead in a lot of different aspects of life. In the bedroom and not. I guess after ten years of that, she'd figured I was a pushover and could get away with anything." I pause to make sure she's still with me.

"So, what happened?" she whispers.

I take a breath. I could get used to the subtle vanilla bean scent of her hair, but it's the fact that her skin gives off that same delicious smell that really gets me. It's the type of scent that sticks in memories for years. It's unforgettable. Just like she is. Something I learned the hard way.

"Well, we were married for just over ten years. And by the end of it, she asked me for an open marriage. By that time, I guess I just didn't give a shit anymore. I knew she was cheating. I'd caught her a few times. I think, by that time, I just didn't think I could do any better. She'd beat me down. Not in the ways that you were, exactly. At least not as viciously. It had gotten to the point where I'd leave in the morning to go to work. She'd still be sleeping. She didn't bother to get up. Didn't do the simple things anymore, like kiss me goodbye or mumble to have a good day. She'd push me away if I tried to hug her. I'd come home at night and eat dinner on my own because she was out somewhere. I'd go to bed by myself. She'd crawl in late at night or early morning, however you want to look at it."

"That's awful…"

"I'm honestly not so sure I would have left had Matt not pushed me. And Mariah. I guess I'd finally had enough. I decided I was better off on my own. The divorce wasn't amicable. She was pissed that I wasn't providing for her anymore. I offered to give her a fair settlement and pay her alimony. Legally, I wasn't obligated to do any of that. She cheated on me and was living with the dude she cheated with. Initially, I'd offered her my fucking house. I offered to pay off her car. Give her spousal support. Give her a settlement. I just wanted her out of my life. I knew she was money hungry. None of it was enough. She got a lawyer. Accused me of physical, mental, and emotional abuse. None of which she had any proof of. No police calls. No witnesses. Even her own lawyer didn't believe her.

I never touched her. I'd never do that shit. But she dragged me through the mud. She went to some of my colleagues and tried to get me fired. It was all a very fucked up, chaotic mess."

"I don't like her."

I chuckle. "She got what was coming to her. Matt and Mariah really rallied around me. They made me really take a second to look at everything she took from me. Which was, basically, my entire identity. It took a little while, but I got myself back. The only real difference was that I refused to ever get back into any kind of relationship again. I was a one night and done kind of man. I wouldn't let the women I took home stay the night. I called them a cab as soon as I was done with them. And, if you want me to be honest, most of them were perfectly happy with the arrangement. I made a habit of not taking home women that struck me as relationship types. They were all young college girls for the most part. Just wanted to have fun and got a kick out of taking a cop to bed. And then, you crashed into me."

"I'm sorry." I feel her finger tips tangle the hem of my shirt into her fist. "I didn't mean to."

"Lyric. Baby, it's not your fault."

She looks up at me. Her eyes are red and puffy and break me. "I wasn't watching where I was going. I ran into you. It was my fault."

I can't help the smile as I shake my head. "It wasn't a bad thing."

She furrows her brows in confusion. "It... wasn't?"

I shake my head again and pull her a little closer. "No. I've never in my life met a woman like you. Your wit is second to none. You're beautiful. You're sexy without even trying. But beyond all of that, Lyric, you made me laugh. Really laugh. Not the forced laugh. Not the polite laugh. I laughed because of you and the fact that you made me. That stuck with me. It stuck with me more than the fact that I couldn't get your voice out of my head. More than your beautiful eyes."

She blushes and hides in my neck. "I thought you didn't like me."

"I know why you thought that, and I'm sorry. I didn't mean to make you feel like that, Lyric. I thought by sending you that text message, I could, somehow, be the hero and save you from me. I didn't want to break your heart. I used your brother and my friendship with him as an excuse, and that was wrong. Luca has been trying to figure out ways to get me to meet you for a long time. I've avoided it because I didn't want you to end up being another girl in a long list of girls. At least that's what I told myself. Truth is, he's told me a lot about you. I didn't want to meet you because I knew you were the relationship type. And furthermore, I think I instinctively knew that you could break me out of my no relationship rule. You're the type of woman I'd want to spend time with."

"So… you…" She trails off.

I can feel her biting her lip. I reach up and run my thumb over it. "Stop biting that beautiful lip."

"Sorry, sir," she says softly as she releases it.

I groan because just those words send all of my blood rushing like the rapids directly to my dick. I can feel it start getting hard before I have any hope of stopping it. I shift her slightly without making her feel like I'm pushing her away. I don't want her to feel that. Not again. But I also don't want her to feel my growing issue.

"I'm trying to say that I do want to spend time with you, Lyric. And I'm apologizing for being an asshole and trying to push you away before I got to know you. I'm sorry for giving you my number, and then sending you a rash text that I didn't mean and only sent because of my own fears. I didn't know how it would make you feel. I'm sorry I made you feel unwanted, and that you did something to upset me. Nothing could be further from the truth. You didn't do anything wrong."

"I texted you a lot…"

"I wasn't upset by them. Actually, seeing your name was the highlight of my day. I found myself looking forward to it. It's a little scary to want to be in this position again. To want to try again, and be with the same woman more than once."

"You're… not mad at me?"

I chuckle and shift her so she's straddling me. "Come here," I say quickly when she sits back a little. I grip her hips and slide my hands up to her waist. I wrap my arms around her and pull her close. I relax a little when I feel her arms wrap around my shoulders. "That's better. Now, look at me."

She looks up at me slowly. I could drown in her eyes and die a happy man. Everything about Lyric is soft. Shy. Hesitant. Submissive, just as Luca said. Just as I instinctively knew. She calls to me in ways no one ever has before. She's managed to awaken pieces of me that I thought were extinct. Just watching her suck on her bottom lip makes me want to both kiss her and slap her ass. The dominant in me I thought I killed a long time ago is fighting to come out.

Part of me wants to let him because I think she'll respond nicely to him. If she's as submissive as Luca said and as what I'm seeing, she needs a dominant to make her feel complete and in control. I've learned at least that much in my life, though I've never really been a true dominant. At least not like women see on TV.

Christian Grey. Fucker makes me want to throw up.

I look at her sternly and narrow my eyes at her lip. She immediately releases it. I take a second to study it. There's no doubt that she spends a lot of time biting it. The skin is broken and chapped. It looks like there's some dried blood almost in the middle of her bottom lip.

I clear my throat to keep my heart from breaking. "Don't bite your lip. It's hurting you. I don't like seeing my girl hurt."

She nods, smiling softly. "Yes, sir. I won't."

"Good girl."

I take a quick moment to look her over as she blushes. Lyric really is small. She's almost underweight. Given how she was treated over the years, I didn't really expect anything different. When I saw her up close and in person at Mariah's party, I wasn't really paying attention to anything other than if she was hurt. Not to say I didn't notice the girl is beautiful. She's incredible. I'd be stupid not to see it. It's difficult not to take all of her in. But she's also very good at hiding things. I've discovered one of them is her body.

"So, you... do... like me?"

I meet her eyes with a smile. "It's impossible not to like you. You've gotten under my skin." I brush her hair gently back behind her ear. "What do you say to giving this a chance? We'll take it slow. Maybe start out with a movie. Your choice. I'll even subject myself to a romantic Hallmark love story."

She scrunches her nose and shakes her head. "No thank you. I vote for Jurassic World."

I laugh. "Thank fucking God for that."

"Followed by Kong: Skull Island."

"A girl after my own heart."

"And snacks. Popcorn with M&M's."

I grin. "Popcorn with M&M's is like food porn."

She giggles before her face falls. "Do you… I mean, would you… be upset with… cuddling?" She looks so hopeful that I can't help the smile that crosses my face.

I tighten my arms around her. "I'd be sad if you didn't want to cuddle with me. Maybe a little heartbroken. Probably dejected." I try to hold back the smile, but it spreads across my face.

Lyric blushes as she giggles. "I'll get the popcorn." She starts to slowly get up.

I let her go and watch her every move, but I miss her next to me. I've never in my life missed someone who is in the same room. I've never wanted them close to me all the time. I've never craved them as much as I do her. It's an obsession. I've always thought obsessions were dangerous. The assumption may be correct, but I'm not so sure I really care right now. The only thing that matters to me is making Lyric feel like she's a Goddess.

Because she damn fucking well is.

She puts the bowl and a couple cans of soda down as she sits. "Oh. I forgot a blanket. You can't watch a movie and snuggle without a blanket."

She starts to get up, but I tug her down. "I got it, honey. Relax."

She smiles shyly and sits. She snuggles into the couch as she watches me. "There's one at the foot of the bed in my room."

I wink as I head for her room. "On it."

I quickly make my way to her bedroom. I can't help but chuckle at how clean it is. Considering her profession, the fact that she's so clean and organized doesn't surprise me. There's nothing out of place.

I grab the blanket and close her door behind me. Lyric is curled up with her arms wrapped around her knees. It's pretty obvious she's still a little unsure of my intentions. I can't really blame her. With everything she's been through coupled with all of her thoughts thanks to my idiotic text message, I'm a little surprised she's even allowing me near her. I wouldn't have been at all shocked if she'd told me to stay the hell away from her. I would have deserved it.

I sit down and spread the blanket over the two of us. She watches me as I settle. I can tell she's still unsure of how to act around me. Her past, like mine, has shaped her actions. She's not all that different from me.

I also know that it's my actions that will reassure her. Without any hesitation, I hold my arm out for her. She looks at it before looking at me and moving slightly closer as she takes a deep breath. She lets go of her knees. I count that as an improvement.

"You can't cuddle with me if you're way over there, beautiful," I drawl with a smile. She moves a little closer, but not where I want her. I pull her closer so she's tucked into my side. "Much better."

She sighs in obvious contentment. Her body relaxes into mine. "I agree."

I kiss the top of her head as she starts the movie. "I'm not like your exes, Lyric. I really have no problems with a beautiful woman tucked into my side while a movie is on. Or at any other time, for that matter."

She nods slowly and shifts a little, turning her body a little more towards mine. She wraps her arms around herself like she's hugging herself, but I feel one of her hands against my side. It's like she's testing me to see how much I'll let her touch me before I push her away. I smile and run my hand up and down her arm.

As the movie plays, though, I pay very little attention to it. All of my focus is on her. What her hands are doing. How relaxed she is. When she giggles, I kiss the top of her head. Before long, I can tell she's feeling better and a little more comfortable by the way she's touching me.

By the time the second movie starts, her hesitancy is nearly non-existent. She's comfortably snuggled into my side. She's smiling and laughing. It's by far the most adorable thing I think I've ever seen.

But it's the touching that starts driving me crazy. Her hand has gone from being against my side to around my waist. She casually rubs my hip for a while before moving her hand to my stomach. She traces my abs as she becomes so engrossed in the movie that she jumps when Kong roars.

I casually drop my hand underneath her arm to cover my growing hard on. The intention here is to help her understand that there is nothing at all wrong with her wanting to cuddle or touch me. But I don't want her to know that just having her near me does things to my body that should be illegal in all fifty states. I have a feeling that would scare her away.

When she starts tracing words on my thigh, though, is when I give in and close my eyes as I give myself a squeeze in hopes of relieving some of the pressure. I'd get up and take care of it, but I don't want to leave her.

The thought of her not being at my side, even for a few minutes, isn't a thought I enjoy at all.

I lean my cheek on top of her head and chuckle a little. I'm certain that any woman I've ever been with would be doing what she's doing intentionally to get some type of a reaction. But not her. Lyric is so obviously oblivious to what she's doing that I can't help but think it makes her even more adorable.

"I thought you'd have to work today."

I jump slightly at Lyric's soft and melodic voice. I wasn't expecting her to say anything. It's the first words she's said since we sat down and got settled. She's laughed. She's jumped a little. She's made cute whimpering noises. When she eats the popcorn with the M&M's she makes sexy as fuck moaning noises that are so soft, I doubt she knows she's making them.

The squeezing of my dick has done nothing to help me. I shift a little, hugging her tighter to me so she doesn't think I'm running away. When she moves her hand from my thigh quickly, probably thinking I don't want it there, I grab her hand and put it back, dropping my hand over my throbbing cock once more.

"I was supposed to. But I took the day off. Talking to you was far more important. I'll be busy tomorrow, but that's an issue for then. Today is about you and making sure that you understand that nothing about what happened was your fault. And making sure you know that I like you and want to try this whole relationship thing again. Words I never thought I'd say, but you make it impossible for me to not want to try again."

She blushes once more with a shy smile before sucking in a breath. "Are you kidding me?" She gives the TV the dirtiest look I think I've ever seen a woman give to anything or anyone. I bite back the laugh. "No! You leave poor Kong alone, you two-faced douchenozzle, overuses the motherfucking word, short-stacked nugget! No! Don't shoot at him! Pick on someone your own size, you teacup scout!"

I glance at the TV after watching her beautiful tangent before I start laughing. "Fucking adorable." I smile at her. Her eyes are riveted to the TV as the team starts their war to take down Kong.

"No! Don't try to blow him up! Leave him alone! Ha! Yeah! You point your guns at the teacup scout. See how you like it, asswipe!"

"I don't know which I like more," I whisper low in her ear. I grin when she shivers. "The movie or watching you watch the movie."

She blushes and ducks her head. Her eyes go wide when the skullcrawler comes shooting out of the water with a boom that makes her jump, even though she seemingly knows it's coming. "Uh-oh... that's a big one... Go Kong!" She watches for a few moments. Her hand grips my thigh. "Oh no... Kong's down..." She frowns at the TV so sadly I wonder if she actually feels the pain. She blinks and tilts her head. "Well, that's not the best time to pause to take a video..." Her eyes widen and she gasps. "No! Big lizard-snake sees them! Time to go! Zoom!" She giggles when the humans start running away.

"How did I ever survive watching this movie without you?" I grin when she blushes again. "So adorable."

"Am not..."

I kiss her blush and tangle my fingers in her hair. "Are so."

She lays her head on my chest. "Can we watch another one?"

"We can do whatever you want. Say the words. I'll make it happen."

Her smile is so bright, she could light the entire room. I decide in this moment that there is nothing more important than her and keeping that smile on her face. She could ask me for anything in the world, and I'd get it for her if it means her happiness.

Chapter Nine

☆ Lyric ☆

(Four Days Later)

I whine petulantly because I simply don't care anymore. If I wasn't worried about being run over, I'd sit on the floor and throw an all-out tantrum. So instead, I settle for stomping my foot against the floor underneath me and crossing my arms over my chest.

Luca, my asshole brother, has the balls to laugh. "Lyric, I can't do anything about it. All I can do now is hope for the best. And you need to prepare for the worst."

I sigh exasperated. "And what could possibly be worse than no servers?"

"Well, the stove could blow up."

My eyes widen. "Don't you jinx it!"

He shrugs. "I could lose the rest of my staff and have to do all of this myself."

"Luca! No!" I cover my ears.

"But my personal favorite… We could lose power. Which would mean no food. No grand ball for Gainesville's finest."

I squeak and cover my mouth. "Stop it! This instant! Get back to work while I figure out how to fix this disaster!"

He mock-salutes me then turns in the most ridiculous way imaginable. I'm about to chastise him for saluting in such a disrespectful manner, but he nearly falls on his ass when he turns. I giggle when he grabs his knee after slamming it into the corner of the counter.

"Fuck me. That hurt like a motherfucker."

"Serves you right for disrespecting the military."

I leave him to stew and rub his knee as I walk out into the ballroom. I need to breathe. Today is my day to shine. It's the day of the Police Grand Ball. My day to really showcase what I can do with a miniscule budget. I've been living and breathing the ball the past four days. After my talk with DJ and my day spent watching movies with him, this ball has been almost the sole thing on my mind.

I'd even saved money and have some left over to give back to Chief King when I see him tonight. It's something I'm beyond excited for. I can't wait to see how surprised he will be that I didn't use everything he gave me.

Of course, the powers that be aren't on my side. Luca just informed me that two of the three people he had coming in to help serve are sick. Well, one of them is sick. The other is her husband and doesn't think he should be around food if he's carrying the nastiness she has. I couldn't agree more, but it helps me none. I can't serve dinner when I'm expected to do literally everything else. Like make sure the band is here and doing what needs to be done.

Which they are not.

"This… can't… be happening." I look up at the ceiling. "Why? Why is this happening? Did I do something? Is it me?"

"Doubtful," a deep and very sexy, rich, Southern accented voice says behind me.

I turn quickly. My heart speeds a little at the sight of DJ leaning against the wall with his arms crossed over his chest and his feet crossed. He's so incredibly handsome. He's wearing blue jeans and a t-shirt, but he looks like a superhero. He's so ridiculously sexy, it really should be outlawed. He should honestly arrest himself.

I try to smile, but it doesn't quite reach my lips. I sigh instead. "I have the worst luck. I really should just give up event planning. Something bad happens at every event I'm involved in."

DJ drops his arms and pushes off the wall. He struts towards me. "I doubt that."

"It's true!" I flail my arms in frustration. "Mariah's party? The chef quit. The sous chef had to take over."

"But the sous chef took over. Crisis was averted. Mariah had a hell of a time."

I narrow my eyes. "Did you know the pipe burst in that room? Matt was there. I had a panic attack to rival panic attacks. He forced me to tell him why I was freaking out. I had to tell him about the bathtub and shower incident." I sniffle.

He narrows his eyes right back at me with a stupidly sexy, panty-soaking smile. "But you dealt with it. Matt was here to help you get through the panic. You made a good friend out of it."

I pout at his uncanny ability to turn everything positive. "A little kid's party last month? The pony pooped on the cake. I had to call the baker and beg her to get me a new one. She couldn't. Even though it was her fault the cake was on the ground in the first place. She left it with all of the party decorations in the grass. I will never use her services again. I had to buy a store-bought cake."

"Did the kid have fun and enjoy the cake?"

I chew on the inside of my cheek. "Yes… And his mother thought it was hilarious."

"So, everything still turned out. Hmm… I wonder why? Maybe because the party planner has a way of fixing shit that's broken." He grips my chin and tilts my face up so I'm looking at him. "Cheek. Biting. Quit it."

I release my cheek instantly. "Sorry, sir," I say submissively.

He leans down and kisses me. He smiles as he pulls away slowly. "Good girl." He slides his arm around my waist and pulls me close. His body is so hard and warm. Safe. "Now. Tell me what's going on. How can I help?"

"Oh no." I shake my head. "You're the police. This ball is supposed to be for you."

"Actually… no. Yes, the Officer of the Year is announced. Other awards. But above all else, this ball is a fundraiser. The money goes to our foundation. Which ends up back in the community. Like, for example, it's a hundred degrees out and grandma's air conditioner breaks. She calls for help because she's homebound. She doesn't know what to do. She has no family to help her. She's scared. I would buy her an air conditioner and bring it to her. It's an emergency, so I wouldn't have time to get the approval for it. But I can turn in the report and my receipt and get reimbursed for it. We can also use that money to help the single mom on the street with a flat tire. We can get her a tire, or help with the tow if something else is wrong. We can do a lot of things with that."

I didn't think it was possible, but he's managed to make me have more feelings for him. He's so kind and generous. I've learned that over the past few days. The other night, he took me to dinner and a movie. We walked from the restaurant to the movie theater, and DJ saw two people on the way who were sitting on the sidewalk with signs about needing money for food. He didn't break conversation with me at all, but he stuck two twenties in each of their hands. They both started crying when they were thanking him. He told them both to have a good meal as he walked along with me.

"You have such a kind heart," I say as I hug him.

"I have my moments." He kisses the top of my head before pushing me just enough away so he can look in my eyes. "Now, tell me what's going on."

I sigh and let my arms fall to my side. I turn a little towards the kitchen. "Luca is doing amazing. But two of the three people he had volunteering to help serve are sick."

"Well, that's not too bad."

"It's a disaster, DJ. I can't find people this close to the event to cover. And to get them to volunteer their time? That's even more difficult."

"Well, I -"

"The sous chef. He's out. He decided it was too much work to volunteer his time," Luca says when he comes out of the kitchen. He holds his hands in front of him as if he's warding off evil. "Before you say it, I'm sorry. I shouldn't have said it."

I just look at him a few moments while I blink. Finally, I take a deep breath. "If I could scream right now, I would. But I can't. So, I quit. I'm done. The universe hates me. I'm going home."

"No, no, no," DJ says as he pulls me into his arms when I try to walk by him. "There will be no quitting. This is what you love doing. And you're fucking phenomenal at it." He kisses the top of my head. "I'll take care of the servers. How many do you need? Two?"

I nod into his chest as my head spins in too many different directions to keep up. "How does this happen to me? Do I attract it?"

"Lyric. Stop. Look at me," DJ commands. My eyes snap to his as I rub my chest. "I have the servers. I'll take care of it. Do you have any contacts for a sous chef? Because if you don't, I'll take care of that, too."

I shake my head. "I don't. I really don't. The people we usually work with expect payment. I can't think of anyone who would do this on this short of notice for nothing. And even if I called them, I don't have enough left to cover their payment. DJ -"

"Lyric." He takes my face in his large hands. I melt into the rough calluses I've come to adore and close my eyes. "Trust me. Let me help."

I nod slowly as I blink back tears. "I don't want to fail. I have five hundred dollars written on a check that I want to give back to Chief King. I didn't use it. I really don't want to. I know one sous chef, but there's no way he can be here on such short notice, and his fee is more."

"Ssh…" DJ kisses me softly and takes my hand. He looks at Luca. "Keep doing whatever you're doing. I'm on the help thing."

He nods. "Got it." He spins and nearly runs back to the kitchen.

"What are you going to do?" I whisper.

He kisses my hand and leads me to a table. He sits me down and takes a seat next to me. "I ended up being pretty good friends with a couple of my one-night stands."

I watch as he takes out his phone. "So… you're calling one of them?" I look down and play with my fingers.

"Baby." He leans in and kisses my cheek. "There's nothing between me and any of them. I have no problem telling you that you're the only one I want over and over again if that's what you need from me. But we have a problem. I have contacts that can help. They can't be considered exes because we never had that kind of a relationship. They are friends. Not friends I hang out with on a daily basis, but periodically, yes. I will speak with them. Usually, it's when one of us needs a favor. Like when one of my one-night stands wants more. Then I use one of them to fake being my girlfriend. I'm only too happy to do the same for them. We'd do anything to help each other out. But we're not close enough to talk to each other all the time."

I smile and nod slowly. That does make me feel a lot better. His thumbs gently rubbing the back of my hands also helps. He leans in and kisses the tip of my nose. I wiggle it with a giggle. He smiles.

"I guess we should probably call them then. They need to be here soon so Luca can give them direction."

"You got it." He gives me a wink as he starts dialing a number. He leans over and kisses me as he puts the phone to his ear.

I blush and duck my head because the entire time he's talking, his eyes are on me. It's hard to miss the complete adoration shining in them. It makes his eyes sparkle and a little darker of a green. He's so beautiful. And he's all mine.

It's still a little strange to me to use those words. I feel like it's presumptuous to call him mine when I'm not really even sure exactly what we are. Everything is still so new, and I don't want to come off too needy and push him away. It's why I find myself hesitant to touch him, kiss him, even hug him unless he does it to me first.

He hangs up the phone and kisses my hand. "Servers are dealt with and one of them is bringing her uncle… who is a sous chef."

"I love you. Really." I cover my mouth as my eyes go wide. "I'm so sorry. I shouldn't have said that… I… should not… have said… that." I mumble behind my hand. Oh God. How? How could I do that? The number one way to make a guy run is to say something stupid like that.

"Lyric," DJ whispers. He wraps his hand around my wrists and gently tugs. I resist and keep my hands firmly placed against my mouth. He smiles and leans forward. He kisses both of my hands. "Lyric, I'm not running away. See? I'm still here."

"That was so stupid of me to say."

DJ narrows his eyes and pulls my hands a little harder. I have no choice but to drop them. I lower my eyes. I expect the worst. Like him to say he doesn't feel that way about me. That it's too fast.

But that isn't DJ.

He slowly stands and pulls me up with him. He takes one of my hands in his and turns, pulling me towards the bathrooms. I follow with my eyes on the floor. I nervously chew my lip because I have no idea what he's doing. The only thing I know is he said he isn't running, and I believe him.

I glance up when DJ pushes a door open and squeak when he pulls me into the men's bathroom. I don't have a chance to protest, though. He lets the door close behind us and spins me around so I'm facing the mirror over the sink. He pushes me just firmly enough to make me grip the counter as I bend over.

"There are two things I will not tolerate you doing, Lyric. The first is biting your lip or cheek. Which you're doing right now. Stop. You're hurting yourself. I won't tolerate it."

I obey without hesitation. "Sorry, sir," I whisper. I blush in shame. I know he hates when I bite my lip.

"It's a form of self-harm. You only do it when you're punishing yourself for something you think you've done wrong, or when you're thinking so hard about something that happened, and you start blaming yourself for it. It's a way to punish yourself, and I'm not allowing that shit. If you want a punishment to ground you or something, you come to me. Understand?"

I nod and look at him through the mirror. "I understand."

"The second is when you talk down about yourself. I happen to think you're pretty fucking spectacular. I won't allow you to call yourself stupid. I'm not going to let you pick yourself apart and find things about yourself to criticize. It's not happening. Understand?"

"Yes, sir." Tears start to fill my eyes because I know I disappointed him. I hate that I did that.

"I'll let you go with just a warning on the lip biting. Do it again, you get five spankings. Understand?"

"Yes, sir. I do," I whimper.

"But I'm not letting you calling yourself stupid go." Without warning, his hand comes down hard across my ass. "Five spankings. Count, little girl."

I clamp my hand over my mouth to stifle the scream as my eyes widen. "One, sir!" I keep my hand over my mouth as his hand slams down on my ass again. "T-two, sir!" I close my eyes against the tears of shame at upsetting him. He slaps my ass again. "T-three, sir!" I know it's a punishment, but for some reason, I start to feel a little more centered. Grounded, just as he said I would. It's as startling as it is calming. I wipe my eyes with my other hand as he gently rubs my ass.

"Tell me why you're getting spankings."

I slowly take my hand away from my mouth. "Because I c-called myself stupid."

"Good girl." He slaps my ass again, just as hard as the other three times.

"F-four, sir," I say quietly with a sniffle.

"Tell me why I have a problem with that."

"Because you don't think I'm stupid..."

"And...?"

I frantically try to think of the words, but I can't. "Um... I..."

"Because you aren't stupid, Lyric. And you will stop thinking you are," DJ says calmly, but somehow, still dominantly. The tone calms me almost as much as the spankings. He slaps my ass again, this time leaving his hand on my ass.

"F-five, sir." I blink a few times and sniffle.

DJ pulls me up gently and slowly turns me so I'm facing him. He drops both hands to my ass and rubs the sting of the spankings away. He leans down and kisses me with such love and passion that I nearly forget my name. I close my eyes and let his kiss wash away the remainder of the self-doubt the spankings didn't obliterate. My racing mind slows. I feel calmer. Not so out of control.

DJ pulls away slowly but keeps me flush against him. He squeezes both of my ass cheeks. "I don't like resorting to spankings. I only do it when I feel like it's the only way to get my point across. I don't like punishments, Lyric. But as I learn more about you, it seems like this is what you respond to. Am I wrong?"

I shake my head and look up at him. "No... I feel... calmer. More grounded... like you said. I... I feel like it brings me down. I feel less out of control." I shake my head slowly. "I'm not sure I'm explaining right."

"You are. Keep talking. Tell me. I need to know that you're getting what you need out of me. In all aspects of the relationship. Not just when you're feeling like you need to be held or need to talk. My job here is to give you everything you need."

I take a breath as I try to formulate my words. "I've always felt… submissive. Like I need someone in my life to take control and both lead and guide me. I don't like decision-making. I don't do well…" I pause as I think. "Um… I don't do well with decision-making. And I don't mean just in the bedroom. I mean, like, in life. I'm just a submissive person. Not weak or…" I sigh and pause again. "I hate words."

"Lyric. Stop thinking. Just tell me."

I use his strength to give me a little of my own. "I'm better in a dominant-submissive relationship. It's why I tend to call you sir in certain situations. Not like BDSM. Gross. I refuse to be tied up and gagged. I do like the control not being in my hands, though. I've just never… trusted… anyone enough to… um… to really give up total control. And that makes me panic a little because I don't like being the one in control." I deflate slightly. "Does that make sense?"

He grips my ass and picks me up. He sets me on the counter and places both of his hands on the counter on either side of me. "You're a submissive by nature. A natural submissive. There's nothing wrong with that. You prefer a dominant man. An Alpha, if you want to use that word. You like to have fun in the bedroom, but you don't like to feel completely like the control is taken from you. Which, given what you've been through, I can't blame you. I'd say you're a little tired of hiding who you truly are because you're afraid to be judged. And I'd say you're also a little afraid to admit that because of your past. When you did allow yourself to let go a little bit, you ended up in situations that you should have never been subjected to. You feel like it's your fault for letting your guard down. So, you're afraid to really trust enough and allow yourself to be who you are. Which makes you feel out of control and out of sorts. How am I doing so far?"

I blink. "Spot on, actually."

He smiles and kisses me softly. "I am not walking away because you said you love me. I don't know if I'm ready to tell you I love you back, but I will say this. I have never felt this way about anyone. I have never trusted that I could truly be myself because, like you, I'm afraid of being judged. With you, though, I feel like I can be who I am. I want you to feel that same way about me." He runs his thumb over my lower lip. I lower my eyes and look up at him through my lashes. "Think you can give me a bit of time to figure out if what I feel is love? Since I've never felt that before?"

I nod slowly. "I really didn't mean to say that."

"And I really don't mind that it was said, honey. But I'm not going to say it back unless I know the words coming out of my mouth are the truth. This is still very new to me. I don't want to fuck anything up. I've never wanted to spend time with anyone like I do you. I've never missed someone when I don't have my arms around them. Until you, Lyric, I've always been content to kick a girl out after I finish. My marriages were exactly the same. I didn't give a shit if they wanted to cuddle or not. It made no difference to me. I'm not used to feeling the need to constantly be around someone like I do you. Is it love? Probably. But I need to work that out, sweet girl." He kisses me softly again. "Okay?"

I nod. "Okay."

"Good girl." He kisses my forehead. Every single fiber of my being sighs in contentment at being called a good girl. It's a feeling I'm not used to but one I'm loving every second of. "Now. The real reason for this talk. I don't ever want to hear you calling yourself stupid again."

I nod. "No talking bad about myself."

"And no self-punishment. Which includes biting that lip."

I nod again. "No self-punishment."

"Good girl. You and I are going to go out there. We're going to do whatever finishing touches you need to do. We're getting through this together. And you, little one, are going to show the entire fucking city just who the best event planner is."

I tilt my head. "I love when you call me little one, but why do you do it?"

He kisses my nose. "Because you're so much smaller than me, and I really fucking love it."

I smile and wrap my arms around his neck when he kisses me deeply. His tongue swipes across mine as he pulls me to the edge of the counter. I can feel his hardened cock against my center, and it takes my breath away. I let out a whimper when he steps back and lifts me off the counter. He lets me down just as slowly as he pulls away from the kiss.

It takes me a moment to come back down to Earth, but when I do, he still makes me feel like I'm walking on the softest of clouds. He leads me back out to the ballroom. I feel lighter. Like, with him, the world just might be on my side this time.

Chapter Ten

☆ *DJ* ☆

(Two Weeks Later)

"So, you're asking me to get a warrant," I say looking down at the folder in front of me.

"Yes, sir."

I put the folder down and close it. I fold my hands on top of it and look at the officer sitting in front of me. "You know I'll fight for you guys. But I can't take this to a judge. You have nothing but circumstantial shit that you have absolutely no proof of."

"But -"

I hold up a hand. "No. I can't do it. You have one person saying that there's a bunch of activity going on. This is a college town. This house is smack dab in the middle of fucking campus housing. There's no way for me to say this is a drug house. For all I know, this could be a party house. You haven't done any surveillance. You're going off the word of a pissed off neighbor. You have enough here to set yourself up on surveillance."

"Captain -"

I shake my head and hand him the folder back. "Out. No one on my team is going to get away with taking the easy way out. That's not why I got into Law Enforcement. It sure as fuck ain't going to be the way I run my team."

"But, sir -"

I narrow my eyes. "I'm not telling you again. Go. Get surveillance on the house. Then come talk to me about warrants. I ain't getting you one only to have you end up running into a party house and having a fucking kid's lawyer father up my ass. Now get out."

The officer sighs as he grabs the folder. "Yes, sir."

I shake my head as I watch him leave. Why the hell he would think to come to me when he has nothing to go on is something I can't quite figure out. I have a reputation for fighting for my officers. But everyone knows that if they don't put in the fucking work, I'm not going to do anything for them. I have enough work to do. Doing the leg work of my cops is never something I will or have ever done.

"Sounds like you've had a tough day, Captain."

I smile at Lyric. She's standing in my doorway wearing skinny jeans that show off more than I think she's aware of and a t-shirt that is a little tighter than I'm sure she thinks it is. Her hair that she somehow manages to put up or back or in braids is falling loosely over her shoulders. She probably thinks she looks conservative and adorable. But to me, she falls more into the sinfully sexy category.

"To what do I owe the honor of my beautiful girlfriend surprising me with something that smells delectable for lunch? And looking quite gorgeous, too."

She blushes. One of my new favorite things is making her blush. The past two weeks with her since the Police Officer's Grand Ball have been incredible. She's starting to come a little out of her shell, and I'm enjoying the hell out of the benefits that come with it.

"I thought I'd surprise you. I brought steak and cheese sandwiches. Homemade. Luca refused to allow me to feed you anything from Subway."

I grin. "So…, Luca. He made them?"

She blushes even darker and looks down. "I helped. I made sure the steak was made the way you like it. And I helped season it. Then I put the sandwiches together."

My grin is plastered to my face. "So fucking beautiful." I stand and walk towards her. I wouldn't think it's possible, but she manages to blush even darker. I gently tug her into my office and close the door behind her. I take her hand and lead her behind my desk. I sit down and pull her in my lap.

"They smell amazing."

"I hope you like it." She leans forward, giving me a perfect view of the cleavage I'm not sure she realizes she has.

"I'm positive I'll love it." I kiss her arm and wrap my arms around her waist as she pulls the sandwiches out.

She giggles when I kiss her neck. "DJ, behave."

I smile against her neck and start nibbling as my hand snakes up her shirt. I grip her side just under her tits. Perfect position for my thumb to run teasingly across her nipple. It hardens immediately for me.

"I always behave. I'm a perfect angel."

She laughs. I love her laugh. It's like music directly to my heart. "So not true. You are the least angelic person I know."

I nip her neck and drop my hand to her thigh. "I'd be insulted, but you're absolutely right."

She giggles again. "Eat now. Playtime later. I know you've been busy. I want you to at least have a nice lunch."

"Yes, ma'am." I dutifully shift slightly and take the sandwich, but I don't miss her shiver or her squeezing her thighs together. She loves when I say those words in my deep Southern accent. It instantly makes her wet. "So, how was your day?"

"Good. I needed the day off. I'm glad I had the opportunity to take it. We've been getting a lot of business since the Grand Ball. I can't even believe it."

I smile. "I can. You did an incredible job, baby. Chief King can't stop talking about it. He tells everyone how incredible you are and what a good job you did. I know you had a lot of volunteers, but you're still amazing at what you do with budgets. I mean, those decorations you made and the centerpieces. No one would have ever guessed those blue and white lilies weren't real. You had real water in there, and real jeweled rocks. The flowers looked real. And they had a scent to them."

She nods and smiles excitedly. I love the way she gets when she's talking about her work. She's so passionate about it. "I have a lily scented spray that I use. I actually have a spray for all of the popular flowers. Like roses and carnations. It was one of my biggest splurges. I bought them myself, though, so they never came out of anyone's budget. The flowers are reusable. And they came out of the budget I was given by the Center for decorations. I have a lot of stuff that's reusable, so unless there's something specific they want, I probably already have something I can use."

"I'm never going to get tired of hearing about your job. I love how much you love it."

She smiles. "I do. I really do. It's something I'm good at and really enjoy. I don't feel like I'm going into work. I feel like I'm just going to do something I love that's fun, and I get paid for it somehow."

I kiss her cheek. "That's how it should be."

"How was your day? I assume busy."

I shrug. "Not really busy. But the stupidity I've been dealing with is something I could do without." I nod towards the door. "The officer you saw leaving wanted a warrant for a house he thinks is a drug house. But he came to me with a statement from a neighbor. She said there was a lot of activity throughout the whole night. It's loud, and a bunch of people come and go. I told him it's bullshit. I can't get a warrant, or fight for one, for him on what he gave me. He didn't do any of his own surveillance. He's going off the word of one person. I'll stick my ass on the line for any of those guys and girls if they need me to if it means the betterment of this city. But no way in fuck I'll do their job for them. Put in the work. Then come see me."

She shakes her head. "I hate when they think they can take advantage of you. They know you'll do anything for them, so they think they can just bring you anything, and you'll deal with it."

I chuckle as I finish my sandwich. "They also know I don't tolerate laziness." I kiss her shoulder as I wrap my arms back around her waist. "But you being protective of me and caring about whether I'm being taken advantage of is sexy as fuck."

She blushes as she puts down the rest of her sandwich. Considering how big it was, I'm shocked that she got through half of it. She kisses me softly. "I just hate the thought of them coming to you and trying to take advantage of your willingness to help."

I give her a squeeze. "Thank you. And if I need help, I promise to call you and sick you on all of them."

She giggles and nods. "Thank you."

I kiss her shoulder again and start cleaning up my desk. "What's your plans for the rest of the day?"

"Um… Nothing, really." She thinks for a moment. "There's a new movie I was thinking of going to see, but I don't want to deal with the crowds on opening night."

"How about we find a movie on Netflix or On Demand at my place tonight? We can order in. I'll get Embers. They have good steaks and some other things I think you'll love."

Her eyes widen. I love when she gets so excited that her beautiful eyes sparkle. "Really?"

"Yeah. Sure. I'll give you my key. You can head over there. Actually, how about you grab an overnight bag of things you want to leave at my house? I have some stuff at yours. This way we don't have to go back and forth with stuff. You can make a copy of the key and keep the copy. I'll text you the alarm code. You can come and go as you please. If you want to, I mean. I don't want it to seem too fast."

She shakes her head. "No. It's not. I'd like that."

I give her a half-smile. "Yeah?"

She nods shyly. "Yeah."

I finish cleaning up my desk before I lean in and kiss her. "Good. I was hoping you'd say that. Now. What do you say to dessert?" I smile wickedly, unabashedly looking her up and down.

She blushes but laughs. "DJ!" She glances at the door. "Someone could come in."

"Makes it all the dirtier." I grip her hips and shift as I stand. I lift her and set her on my desk as she adorably flails and giggles. I grip her ass and pull her to the edge of the desk as I sit back in my chair. I look up at her. "Ever since you let me taste you, I can't get enough. I knew you'd be my one weakness."

She smiles shyly and runs her fingers through my hair. "I was so nervous that first time. I didn't know how to tell you what I wanted without sounding like a slut."

I smile and shake my head. "Baby, you are the farthest thing from a slut. And if you'd like my honesty, I've never wanted anyone the way I want you." I lean forward and kiss her chest before teasingly nipping her nipples as I unbutton the black, painted on jeans.

She moans and spears my hair. "DJ." Her head falls back as I kiss up her throat. I nip and suck lightly, drawing another sexy moan.

"So beautiful," I rumble against her neck while I'm lifting her hips just enough to pull her pants down. I start reaching for panties, but stop. I look down before my eyes make their way up her perfect legs to her bare and visibly wet pussy. I look up at her with a devilish grin. "Were you hoping for my tongue? Is that why you ain't wearing panties?"

"Maybe…" She looks down at me shyly and licks her bottom lip. She's trembling for me. Just like I like it.

"Such a naughty girl." I nip her neck before kissing back down her throat.

I grip her shirt hem and pull it up as I kiss down her body. I groan when I get to her tits. Every part of her is perfect to me. I let my hands fall down her sides until they reach her thighs. I lick and nip her nipples through the thin satin of her bra. Her fingers in my hair tighten as she tugs lightly.

She looks down at me. "DJ. Please… I need you."

I smile, enjoying the tease. "You have me."

She whimpers so adorably, I nearly give in. But what fun would the game be if I just did something like that? I go back to lavishing her nipples over her bra as I allow my hands to wander back up her body. Unable to resist much more torture to myself, I push her bra up, revealing the soft flesh of her tits. When my tongue hits her hardened peaks, she arches into me.

"I'm going to come, DJ. I'm already so close."

I nip her nipple. She jerks into me and tries to cross her legs. But I'm between them. Adapting to her surroundings like a pro, she wraps her legs around me and pulls me into her. Before she can rub herself against me, though, I pull back.

"Such a needy little girl." I look up at her with a smirk so she knows I'm teasing her.

I've been using words like 'needy' and 'clingy' in a teasing manner a lot with her. She's started to get used to them and the way I use them. She knows I'm mocking her exes and the way they made her feel. I don't understand even a little why anyone would think a woman like her is either of those things. I'm perfectly content being the one to show her she's perfect in every way.

Special. So fucking special.

When she whines, I know she can't take the teasing anymore. I finally give her what she wants. I settle between her thighs and lick long and slow, savoring the taste unique to only her. I don't know what exactly it is about her that's so different, but I can't get enough of her. I crave her unlike I've ever craved anyone.

I nip her clit. She clamps one hand over her mouth to stay quiet. The other tugs my hair and pulls me closer to the part wanting me the most. I smile against her pussy and let my tongue make its way down. She's shaking. Her thighs are trembling. She pulses around my tongue and clamps down tight when I dive in and start thrusting.

She bucks into me, moaning behind her hand to stay quiet. I start flicking my tongue against her spot. The spot that I've come to learn makes her come almost instantly. I love how quickly her pussy tightens for me.

"I can't hold back. DJ, please, please let me come. I need to come for you." She pleads and tries to hold back. She claws at my shoulder and grips my neck as she rides my tongue.

I smile and growl low. I know it sends vibrations through her pussy and all through her body. It drives her crazy. "Come for me, pretty girl. Now." I whisper the words, but I say them deep and growly.

She jerks into me and lets go of me completely. She clamps her hands over her mouth to muffle the screams. Her hips buck hard. Her pussy tightens and clenches. With each pulse, she spills her deliciousness into my ready and waiting mouth. I more than happily lick and suck on her pussy while she rides out her orgasm and comes down.

When she stops spasming, I lick slower and slower until I finally decide to pull back. I know my girl. She'd willingly let me make her come all day long if I wanted to. I'd happily do it, too. If I didn't have a meeting to get to.

I pull her up slowly. I wrap my arms around her and look up at her. "Better? Did I relieve that ache?"

She blushes and puts her hands against her cheeks as she nods. "I've never... I mean, no one has ever really cared about... me coming... before."

"Well, I'm not your exes, baby. Things are never going to be like that for you ever again, Lyric." I gently help her off my desk and pull up her jeans. I kiss her stomach as I button her jeans and zip them. "Did you eat breakfast today?"

She nods. "I had a crumpet with butter and strawberry jam."

I raise an eyebrow as I slowly stand. "And?" She knows better than to eat such a little amount. Her eating habits are not at all healthy.

"And a glass of milk. I also had a small bowl of fruit. Grapes, melon slices, and strawberries."

I lean down and kiss her softly. "That's my girl. And the stretches to help with your back. Were you a good girl and got them done?"

"Mmhmm. In the morning when I got up. Before the shower and breakfast."

I smile and run my hands down to her ass. I give her a squeeze as she wraps her arms around me and hugs me. "I'm proud of you."

I can feel the pride coursing through her. Another thing I've learned in the short amount of time I've been with her is that she functions far better with a routine. I've gotten her to start waking up at a certain time, doing stretches to help keep her back from stiffening, showering after her stretches, then eating breakfast. I have her eating lunch at a certain time. Then dinner. And, most importantly, I have her going to bed at a decent hour. I've already noticed improvement in her energy levels.

Another significant change I've noticed is that she has become more confident. Not only in us, but also in herself. She's far less nervous around me. She's better about being more open with me. Most importantly, though, is that she carries herself differently. Her head is held higher. She walks taller. She seems to be more sure of herself. She was always beautiful. Recently, though, she's taken it to a whole new level. She radiates an entirely new light.

As I look down into her eyes, gripping her ass, I'm struck with a thought that nearly bowls me over. Something I've thought a lot about since she said the words to me.

I'm in love with this girl.

Head over heels in love with Lyric Sharpe.

So deeply in love with her that I don't really know when it happened. Maybe it was the very second I saw her when Luca showed me a pic of them together. Maybe it was after learning about her from him.

More likely, though, it happened the moment she ran into my back, and I turned to see her on her ass looking up at me with those sexy, wide, surprised as hell eyes.

I lean in and kiss her neck, burying my face in her hair. "Fuck, I'm so in love with you. You make everything better. My day. My nights. My entire fucking life. You're like a breath of fresh air, Lyric. The sun to my dark world."

I don't have to see her face to know she's as surprised at the words coming out of my mouth as I am. It's striking to me that thinking back, I've never uttered those words to anyone. None of my ex-wives. None of my girlfriends. Besides my parents and family or people I consider family, I have not once uttered those words. I've always refused to do it if I never felt it.

I feel everything with Lyric. All of it. Every single feeling I've kept locked away slams into me with a force I'm not at all prepared for. The need to be around her all of the time. Missing her when she's not in my grasp. Every single second I've spent with her and wished for more time. The overwhelming urge to protect her; take care of her. The desire to show her what an incredible woman she is. Support her in life and all her dreams.

It all makes sense now. She's more than just an obsession I can't get out of my head. I'll never get enough of her. Not just her pussy. *Her.*

"I love you, too," she whispers so softly, I almost don't catch it.

Her words are like the calm to the storm of emotions I can't quite describe that's welling up in my chest. My rib cage suddenly feels too small for my lungs. I hug Lyric tighter and let whatever power she has over me work its magic.

I have no idea where this relationship is going to go, but I know damn well I won't be able to survive without her. She's managed to burrow herself so fucking far under my skin, she's a part of me now.

A part I don't ever want to lose and will work harder than I ever have on anything to keep.

Chapter Eleven

✫ Lyric ✫

(Six Months Later)

Mariah looks at the mess in front of us and blinks. "You…" She trails off, having no idea what to say.

I nod. "I know." I cross my arms over my chest.

"DJ has a rule." Mariah takes another look at the mess.

"Yep." I nod again.

"Hell."

"That's definitely where I'm going if all of this doesn't get cleaned up."

Mariah and I start organizing the papers on the table in DJ's dining room. DJ and I have been together now for almost six months. It's been the best six months of my life. He wasn't wrong when he told me that he's nothing like the assholes I was with in my past. He is worlds beyond them. DJ is what a real man should be.

He's one of the kindest men I've ever met. He's so caring and compassionate, even though he doesn't want people to know. He's perfectly dominant. He's not overbearing or controlling. Even when he thinks he is. He's never been with someone who takes to that side of him like I have. When he tells me to be here at a particular time, I do it because I know he has a reason. And that reason? I am not confident after dark. It's a way for him to know I'm safe.

DJ put me on a schedule. I know that he worries it's viewed as him being controlling. I constantly tell him that I don't think of it like that. It's helping me. He makes me eat three meals a day because, sometimes, I get too into what I'm doing and forget. I've gained some weight and am no longer under the weight I should be. I'm starting to love the way I look now. I'm more comfortable in my own skin.

He checks in with me throughout the day to make sure I've eaten. If I don't answer him after ten minutes, he'll try again. If I still don't, it means a punishment. Five spankings. I know the reason is because he worries. He knows I sometimes zone out or that I fixate on things. Sometimes, my mind wanders, and I start thinking things I know aren't true. Things like DJ is going to get sick of me and leave me. If I forget something, I'll berate myself and get into my own head.

When I do things like that, I ignore things. Like food, the bathroom, my phone, even my job. If he ends up calling the Center, or Luca, or even showing up if I don't answer, he always makes sure I'm okay before he decides if there will be a punishment or not.

But he worries about the punishment. He knows they center me and make me feel more myself and centered. Sometimes, though, he wonders if they make me feel like a child. It's one of his insecurities with our age difference and his past.

He knows I have a habit of putting off shaving, even though hair on my legs, underarms, or pussy feels itchy to me. So, he makes me shave when he notices I need to and can tell I'm putting it off. Usually, I shave once every couple of weeks. I can't stand it much longer than that and start becoming uncomfortable. But I hate shaving.

A couple of months ago, DJ noticed that we've been spending most of our time here, at his house. I have my own key. I know his security alarm code. Most of my stuff is here. I feel home here. Luca has met a girl and has her at our apartment most of the time, so I know he's not alone. DJ asked if I wanted to move in. I basically live here anyway. It seemed like the right move.

As soon as I moved in, he noticed that I wasn't sleeping very well, even with the schedule he'd put in place. He saw right away that the reason is because I get lost in books. Especially on days I work most of the day. Books are my break, and I love reading. I love getting lost in other worlds. It's one of the ways I relax my mind. Especially if it starts racing. It tends to do that a lot when it's quiet. I don't like when it's quiet. I never have. The silence allows my anxiety to work me into a tizzy over things that really mean nothing.

Sometimes, though, I lose myself in my reading, and I don't realize what time it is. I end up staying awake long into the night. Even all night. DJ put a stop to that. He knows how much I love reading and knows that, sometimes, I'm just not tired when we go to bed. If he is, he allows an hour before it's lights out. If I go over that hour, it's a punishment. He'd never not allow me to read, so the punishment is five spankings.

One of the biggest rules he's put in place, though, is something that he thinks makes him look like a possessive asshole. To me, though, it proves just how caring and loving DJ is. Whenever I leave the house, I am to wear either his hoodie or one of his t-shirts sprayed with his cologne. Most would think it's to show I'm his. Like it's a possessive move and some way to control me. But that's not what it is in the slightest. His scent calms me. He knows that if he can't be around when anxiety hits, his scent will help.

Which brings us to now. I pull DJ's favorite t-shirt up to my nose and breathe him in. Mariah and I are in the den of mine and DJ's house. It got a little warm, so we turned on the ceiling fan to blow the air from the central air system a little more.

Only… we didn't realize that the fan was on high. Or that it was broken. It's currently hanging precariously from the ceiling. The neat stack of papers I had on the table, along with all of my decorations, glitter confetti included, are everywhere.

It wouldn't be that bad if the place cards and glitter confetti hadn't blown everywhere. The den looks a little like a hurricane hit. Or a tornado. Either one. And his rule. He hates messes as much as me. He expects the house to stay clean. Not that it can't look lived in. But leaving cups or garbage around is a big no-no. The rule applies to all visitors as well as us. Pick up after ourselves. It's a rule I am one-hundred percent behind.

Looking at the mess isn't so bad. It's the ceiling fan that has my heart racing. It could fall at any moment and ruin the solid red oak dining room table. It's the only thing DJ has of his mother's. He loves this table. I can't blame him. It's beautiful.

And it's in danger of being destroyed. All because I made the stupid mistake of turning on the fan. "This is bad," I whisper.

Mariah's eyes widen. She drops the papers and wraps her arms around me. "Breathe, Lyric," she whispers calmly in my ear. "Close your eyes. Take a deep breath. With me, okay?"

I do as I'm told and close my eyes. I take a deep breath and let it out slowly. "I hope he gets here soon. We need to move this table."

"See? Taking a second to regain your composure is always the best option. Now, let's get the remainder of this stuff off the table. Then we can move it."

I shake my head. "No. The table comes first. It's important to DJ. It was his mum's. It's all he has of her."

Mariah nods. "Then grab an end."

The circular table, though, is far heavier than either of us imagined. When DJ gets home, followed closely by Matt, Mariah and I are still grunting and groaning as we move it. Shoving it across the carpet is hard, but lifting it is even harder.

"Jesus fuck. What the hell happened?" DJ asks in alarm.

I jump and spin with a small squeak. "I didn't know the fan was broken. It got hot! We were starting to think the central air system was broken."

DJ and Matt quickly move Mariah and I aside and move the table with such little effort, I'm in awe. I'm constantly in awe of DJ's and Matt's strength. Between the two of them, I'm sure there's nothing they can't move. Even a mountain if they set their minds to it.

As soon as the table is moved, DJ looks up at the fan. "Matt, go get the ladder out of the garage. Mariah. Breaker box. In the basement. Shut off the breaker labeled with a four. Take Lyric. Go."

I scurry after Mariah when she takes my hand and pulls me along with her. DJ keeps his eye on the fan as he kneels and starts picking up the papers and glitter confetti that ended up on the floor. I blink back tears. I'm sure he's disappointed in me. He hasn't looked at me since he saw the fan.

He glared as he looked at it. I can tell he's angry with me. I can feel it. As I watch Mariah shut the breaker off, I wipe my eyes.

Mariah turns and hugs me. "It's okay. I promise."

I nod and allow her to lead me back upstairs. It only takes a few minutes for Matt and DJ to get the fan taken down. In the end, nothing is destroyed. DJ calls someone to deal with the fan and central air. Most importantly, though, the table is okay.

Matt hands me the pile of place cards as he sits down. "Quite the scare, huh?"

I nod, but keep my eyes on the table and my work. I take the place cards. DJ sits next to me. Mariah is on the other side of me. Matt is across from me. I take a deep breath and start sorting the place cards.

DJ drops a hand on my thigh. "Baby, it's okay. You're safe. Mariah is safe. That's all that matters to me."

I look up at him sadly. "I almost wrecked your mum's table…"

He smiles and leans over to kiss the corner of my mouth. "But you didn't." He runs his fingers through my hair and gently tugs. I look over at him. "I care much more about you than this table, Lyric."

"I'm so stupid. I shouldn't have turned on the fan." I inhale sharply as soon as the words are out of my mouth. I snap it shut and look at him, horrified at what I just said.

DJ, never missing anything, narrows his eyes. "Upstairs." His voice is deep. Commanding. He leaves no room for argument.

"Yes, sir," I say quietly.

I immediately stand and walk up the stairs with my head lowered. DJ doesn't move. I don't look back at Matt or Mariah. I don't want to see the disappointment on any of their faces. I take a breath and sit on the bed, waiting for DJ. I can hear him on the stairs. When he gets to the door, I look down at my toes.

I can hear him take a deep breath as he closes the door. "Baby…"

I can hear the disappointment dripping from his voice. I sniffle as I look up at him. "I'm sorry," I whisper.

He kneels in front of me and takes my hands. He kisses them tenderly. "What's my rule?" He looks up at me.

I sniffle at the hurt I see written all over him. "Not to talk down about myself."

He nods. "And what did you just do?"

"I said I was stupid. I talked down about myself."

"Do you know why this is a rule?"

I think for a moment before opening my mouth and closing it again. I take a deep breath. "Because you don't like it."

He gives me a sad half smile as he shakes his head. He squeezes my hands and kisses them again. "Because it hurts me, Lyric." His voice cracks as he looks up at me. "Because knowing you think so little of yourself cuts me open."

My heart breaks. I can feel it implode in my chest. I let out a strangled sob because I didn't know that. I never want to hurt him. "I'm so sorry. I didn't know."

He wraps me in his arms. "I love you. So, so much, honey. I hate that you think what you say or think is stupid. Or that you are." He kisses my neck. "It hurts me so much because you aren't. You're smart. You're such an incredible woman. Just because something happens doesn't mean that you're the cause of it. It doesn't mean your actions make you a stupid person. You and I don't spend a lot of time in the den." He pulls back slowly but keeps his arm around me as he sits next to me. He looks down at me while keeping me securely snuggled into his side. "How would you know anything about the fan unless I told you?"

I look up at him shyly. "I wouldn't."

"Exactly." He leans down and kisses me lovingly. He pulls away slowly. "I'm not going to spank you. This time. The reason is because I think knowing that it hurt me is punishment enough. I can tell you feel bad about it. I think that's worse than a spanking."

I start to bite my lip, but stop myself. Instead, I turn and hug him. I sigh in relief when he puts his other arm around me and kisses the top of my head as he hugs me close. He rests his chin on the top of my head and runs his hand up and down my back.

I sniffle. "I didn't mean to hurt you." I tuck my fingers in his waistband and grip it.

"It's okay. I'm okay. You didn't know."

I nod and close my eyes. I breathe in the intoxicating scent that is DJ. I nuzzle his jaw. After a few moments of holding me until I feel less shaky, DJ starts to untangle me from him. I look up at him, slightly confused. He smiles and kisses my nose as he silently and slowly starts pulling his t-shirt off of me.

I watch him curiously. Matt and Mariah are still downstairs, as far as I know. I feel like we should probably be getting back to them, though I'd much rather stay in DJ's arms the rest of the night. The reassurance would mean everything to me. It would stop my mind from going crazy. Like it's doing now. I know DJ loves me. He shows me and tells me every single day. Yet knowing I hurt him is killing me.

DJ kneels in front of me and kisses from my chest down to my belly button. He undoes the button of my shorts quickly and tugs them down while he kisses back up to my tits. He nips my nipples over my bra.

I drop my head back on a moan. "What are you doing?"

"I know my girl." He nips my other nipple.

"Oh… DJ…," I moan as I close my eyes. My stomach flutters, like it always does, at being called his. I arch my chest into his mouth.

I can feel him smiling. His hands make their way up my legs and sides until he reaches the hooks of my bra. He kisses my neck and unhooks the clasp of my bra like a pro. I tilt my head to give him more access to my neck.

"How's that guilt coming?" He nips then sucks the sensitive skin on my neck.

I giggle. "It's starting to dissipate."

I feel his sexy smile against my neck. "Not good enough." He wraps his arms around me and pulls me with him into the bed.

I squeak and giggle. "What about Matt and Mariah? And Luca will be here soon."

"Matt and Mariah can entertain themselves." He straddles me and takes off his shirt. "Luca is a big boy. I'm pretty sure he can find something to do."

I stare in awe of my boyfriend. I swear he was built and sculpted of steel. Someone carved him. I'm sure of it. No real man looks like he does. His abs are so well-developed that anyone would think he spends all day in the gym. But it's his arms that make me drool. I reach up and trace the muscles of his arms as he unbuttons his jeans.

DJ leans down and kisses me. It turns heated so quickly, it takes my breath away. I gasp as he spears his tongue against mine and dips two fingers into my pussy. My fingernails dig into his arm. My hips jerk up into his hand. He thrusts hard, deep, and fast because he knows that's how

I like it. He sets his thumb against my clit and rubs at the same pace he thrusts.

I ride his fingers and suck on his tongue while holding onto him for dear life. He twists his fingers and crooks them. I don't know where he learned how to do half the things he does, but holy fuck, I love every second of it.

"DJ! Oh my God…" I arch more into him. My pussy tightens around his fingers. I try to hold on, but I know he's about to send me careening over the edge in seconds. "DJ, please!"

He gives me an evil grin and slowly pulls his fingers out. He brings them both to his mouth and sucks me off them. "So fucking sweet."

I pout as I pant. "DJ…"

"Patience, sexy girl." He moves to my side and strips his jeans and underwear.

I unashamedly reach for his beautiful, long, hard, thick cock. The first time I saw it, I had no idea how it would fit inside me without tearing me apart. DJ is a perfect nine inches. I grip him and start stroking, but he grabs my wrist.

I whimper as I watch him. "DJ…" I lick my lips.

He kisses my wrist. "I'm not coming in your hand. And no way in all of fuck are you coming on my fingers."

He settles between my legs and takes my other hand. He pins them above my head while he kisses me and slides his dick slowly and deeply into me, stretching me deliciously. I close my eyes and moan into the kiss, submitting completely to him.

His thrusts begin slow and deep. I wrap my legs around his waist and meet each and every one. I clench around him as he thrusts, making him moan for me. He kisses down my jaw to my neck. With one hand, he holds my wrists. With the other hand, he grips my ass and pulls me up into him.

He kisses down to my nipples and sucks each of them hard before lavishing them both in turn. His thrusts quicken but stay hard and deep. I pant and squirm under him, trying to get as close as I can.

"How's that guilt thing now?" he growls against my nipple before nipping it. He thrusts hard again and again.

I push against his wrists, but I know I'm not getting loose. Not unless he wants me to. "So close…" My pussy pulses erratically around him.

He lets go of my wrists. My hands fly to his back and scratch across his broad shoulders. I arch into him and pull him down with my legs as he thrusts. DJ wraps his arms around me and kisses me long and deeply. His tongue starts a war that he dominates completely.

He rolls his hips against mine. The shockwaves of pleasure he sends into me make me scream. When his hand tangles in my hair, my body has no option but to follow suit. I spear his hair with one hand and dig my other hand into his shoulder. He nips my tongue and reaches between us. He pinches my clit before flicking it. He starts rubbing it in time with his thrusts.

"Ah! DJ!" The sensation of his touch mixed with his searing kiss and the dominance his dick has over my pussy is too much. I'm sent careening into oblivion. My thighs tremble. My body shakes. My pussy vibrates and tightens. I can't form words. All I can do is plead with him through my eyes to let me come.

He grunts and moans as he slams into me. "Come for me, beautiful girl. Now. Right now."

My head falls back on its own accord. "Ah! DJ, yes! Yes! Oh, fuck yes!" My hips jerk hard against him. My pussy clenches around him, squeezing him as I pulse for him.

Like he always does, DJ waits until I start coming before he buries himself inside me. He comes hard with a loud moan against my mouth. "Holy Christ. Lyric! Fuck!" His dick slams into me as he fills me, then he slows his thrusts to help us both through.

A few moments later, he falls on top of me as we both start coming down. We both bury our faces in each other's necks and pant as we hold each other. He doesn't pull out. He knows I'm not ready to lose the contact. I love feeling his weight on me and him inside me.

It takes us both a little time to detach from one another. DJ pulls out slowly while kissing me deeply. I instantly miss the contact and warmth of him when he moves to my side. He smiles and takes my hands. He gently pulls me up. He leads me to the bathroom to clean up. We quickly get dressed, but before he leads me back downstairs, he stops me at the door.

"Be honest. Do you feel better? More reassured that I'm not angry with you or upset with you?"

"I'm okay. I feel better. Really. I do. I feel more… reassured. Comforted."

He studies me for a few moments before taking my hand. "Okay. I don't want to hear anymore of you talking down about yourself."

I nod. "Yes, sir."

He kisses my hand. "Tell me why you didn't get spanked this time."

I look up at him with confidence. "Because you feel like me knowing it hurts you when I talk down about myself is punishment enough."

"Good girl. I'm not going to let it go next time, though, Lyric. I'm hoping that knowing how I feel about it will be deterrent enough."

"Yes, sir."

He leans down and kisses me. "Good girl."

I blush. I love when he calls me a good girl. I always used to think something was wrong with me. What kind of woman likes being dominated? Why does a spanking make me feel better? DJ has helped me learn there's nothing wrong with me.

As he leads me down the stairs, I smile shyly. I never used to feel good enough. I always felt at a lower level than the guys I was with. DJ never makes me feel like that. He's learned me so well over the past six months that I have no idea how I ever lived without him. He's the part of me I looked for but was never able to find. It's like it was always out of my grasp. I was made for him.

When we reach the den, DJ pulls me in his lap. I don't need to tell him that I'm not ready to lose the closeness. It's one of the things that's always made me feel needy and clingy. But DJ never makes me feel like my needs are too much for him. He'll never know what that means to me.

Matt grins, like he knows far too much. "Feeling better?" He winks at me. I blush furiously.

Mariah laughs and elbows him. "Stop it."

Luca, who arrived while DJ and I were upstairs, raises an eyebrow. "I don't want to fucking know, mate."

DJ laughs. "I have no intention of telling you the things I do to your sister."

"Thank fuck," Luca says. He goes back to working on arranging the place cards by table number.

I can't help but giggle. The event all of this stuff is for is a wedding for one of Gainesville's most prominent families. The bride is infatuated with the Historical Thomas Center. She has been since she was a child. Her dream was to be married in the Center. With pink glitter confetti and a live band. I'm happy to make all of her dreams come true.

I smile at the people around the table as they all dive into projects I'd given them before the fan fiasco. I'm beyond honored that they're willing to help me. Beyond Luca, everyone sitting here has come to mean the world to me.

Luca is, obviously, my twin, but also an incredible friend. DJ is the love of my life. Matt and Mariah are the best friends I've always wanted but never had. Everyone sitting here are truly incredible people.

My family.

Chapter Twelve

☆ DJ ☆

(One Week Later)

The woman standing in front of me is truly awe-inspiring. The flowing white gown she's wearing hugs every single curve of her body and accentuates all of her features in the most beautiful way. She's wearing a light brown sparkly flower in her hair that brings out the deep brown of her eyes. There are rhinestones in her dark-brown, wavy hair that catches the light and bathes her in a glow that makes her look angelic.

"So…? How do I look, Uncle DJ?"

I grin. "Beautiful. Really. Joel is a very lucky man, Alicia. Very lucky."

She blushes. Alicia King is my adopted niece. Truthfully, she's the adopted niece of the entire department. Alicia is the Chief of Police's daughter. She grew up around us. Chief King would often take her to work with him just because she was interested in everyone. She took an interest in what he did for a living. It wasn't unusual to see his little girl running around headquarters saying hi to everyone and delivering cookies or treats she'd made with her mother the night before.

But it was me that she really took a liking to. I never really knew why, but I think it probably had a little to do with the fact that, even if I was working the street, I'd come in for lunch and take her with me wherever I chose to go. We'd formed a pretty unbreakable bond. By the time she hit her teenage years and started high school, it had become tradition. We'd go to lunch every single day. She'd tell me about her day and everything she was into at the time.

It never felt odd to me, though it probably was to anyone who knew anything about us. The King family is one of Gainesville's most prominent families. Chief King is the first African American Police Chief in our department's history. Many think it's because of his family and their connections, but anyone who has worked with him knows his skills are unparalleled. He deserves the head job with our department more than anyone.

I didn't come from money. So, when Alicia and I started this relationship we have, many looked at it as me trying to get in good with her father. He wasn't Chief then, but he was well on his way. Truthfully, it was never like that. I just thought his daughter was adorable, and I loved answering all of her curious questions. I still do.

When she met Joel, she was so excited about her relationship with him. I couldn't help but be excited for her. She talked about him like he was the greatest thing that has ever happened to her.

One thing that's always bothered me, though, is that I've never met the guy. I've asked to meet him, but she's always said things like he's really busy. She knows I'm a good judge of character. It made me start wondering if maybe she didn't want me to meet him.

I've pushed it aside as much as I can. I've even tried to quench my curiosity by asking her dad about the guy that stole Alicia's heart. He seems to think he's a good person, so I've let it go, but I still don't like that I haven't met him. Especially when after a very short time, she came to me with a ring on her finger and asked me to walk her down the aisle since her dad is officiating.

After talking to Chief King about it, I agreed, but only because he convinced me that seeing his daughter walk down the aisle towards the man of her dreams is much better than walking her down the aisle and missing out on how beautiful it will be seeing her walk down it with his own eyes.

"I hope everything is ready. It's almost time," Alicia looks towards the door nervously. Her chocolate brown eyes fill with worry.

I chuckle. "Alicia, trust me. Your event planner is second to none. Everything is ready. I promise."

She hugs herself. Her caramel skin erupts in goosebumps. "Maybe you could go check?"

I grin. "Check in with the girl of my dreams? That's not much of a chore."

She laughs and playfully shoves me. "Go! And report back. And make her fix your tie! It's crooked."

"Yes ma'am," I tease as I walk out the door.

Mrs. King, Alicia's mother, is just about to walk in. "How is she? Ready?"

"She's a little nervous. Might need a little motherly love."

Mrs. King laughs. "It's almost showtime. I don't know where you're going, but ten minutes."

I wink. "Yes, ma'am."

I hurry to the ballroom of the Historical Thomas Center, which has been transformed into some kind of magical winter wonderland theme. Lyric has something that looks like ice crystals everywhere. I can't help but turn in a circle in complete awe. When I complete my slow circle, I see Lyric standing a couple of feet away watching me.

"It looks fucking incredible in here," I say raspily. Who knew a guy like me could be touched enough to choke up by wedding decorations?

Lyric smiles shyly, albeit watery. Emotional. "Thank you. The things I can do when there isn't a budget limit."

I smile and walk the short distance towards her. She's putting on a happy exterior, but I know my girl. She's barely holding it together, but I don't know what's wrong. I wrap her in my arms, immediately feeling her tension. She's practically trembling as I look down at her.

"What's wrong?" I kiss her forehead. She bursts into a waterfall of tears I have no hope of stopping. "Fuck. Baby, what's going on?" I glance around and quickly steer her away from prying eyes.

Lyric takes my hand as she tries to wipe her eyes and leads me out of the ballroom. She points to a large sign with the bride's and groom's names. "It's him!"

I stare at the sign, bewildered. She curls into my arms and starts crying again. I glance around and quickly move her to a private hallway with a door I hope leads to somewhere that doesn't have people. I duck into the room, thankful there isn't anyone in it. It looks like a walk-in coat closet or something. I feel for a switch and turn it on.

I whip my head around when I feel a hand on my back, pushing me into the coat closet. I take a breath when I see Luca. He closes the door behind us. The scowl mixed with ferocious glare on his face confuses me even more.

"The fuck is happening right now?" I ask as I hug Lyric to my chest as tightly and protectively as I can. I run my fingers through her hair.

"Joel Trent. It's Lyric's ex," Luca growls dangerously.

I look at him, horrified, as Lyric bursts into a fresh wave of tears. "Please tell me it's just the same name."

Luca shakes his head. "As soon as she saw the sign that the King family put up, she got nervous. So, she texted me a picture of the sign. She looked at the guest book and saw a lot of other familiar names."

I shake my head. "Wait. How the hell did we not know this? We just spent a week helping her with decorations and place cards. How did we not know who the groom was?"

Luca shrugs. "Lyric wasn't hired by the Trent family. She was hired by the King family. She only met with Alicia and her parents. He was never here. Which makes me think he fucking knew."

I kiss Lyric's head. "I need to talk to the Chief. Now. This wedding is off. I won't allow it to go on."

"Please don't leave me. Please," Lyric begs.

"I didn't intend to, baby. I'm not leaving you alone knowing who is in this building. Not a chance in hell."

"We need to get her out of here, DJ," Luca says.

"No. We need to get you out of here. Lyric is safe with me. It's you I'm worried about. If he starts spouting shit off about you assaulting him, it will fuck with your citizenship. You can't be near him."

"I don't care about me," he starts to argue.

"But she does, Luca. And so do I. You need to leave. Now. I'll take care of this."

He glares a few moments. I hold his glare with one of my own. He knows I'm right. Finally, he does exactly what I want him to. He nods and turns to the door. I lean down and kiss the top of Lyric's head.

"Let's talk to Chief King first. We'll go from there, okay?"

Lyric nods. "I don't feel safe without you around."

"I know. I know, honey. I'm not going anywhere. I promise. I'll keep you tucked into my side." I feel Lyric mold herself to me as she breathes deeply.

I don't need to ask her to know she's breathing in my scent to calm herself. It's both a huge turn on that my scent is all it takes for her to calm down, for the most part, and also a large sense of sadness that she's even put into a situation where she needs to.

Luca opens the door and starts to walk out, but plows right into a man about his height. He's clean shaven and dressed in a tux. Looking at the glittery brown flower on his lapel that matches the one in Alicia's hair, it doesn't take much to deduce that he's the groom.

I feel Lyric instantly tense. The fear follows. She's too scared to even move. Luca, on the other hand, looks like he might rip the man standing in front of him apart. His fists ball at his sides. I can hear the low, dangerous growl escape his throat as I push Lyric slowly behind me. She grips my suit jacket hard in her fists and lays her head against my back as she whimpers.

Luca slowly walks the rest of the way out of the room as Joel backs up slowly. I can see the hint of fear in his eyes that he tries to hide behind the cocky facade. When his back hits the wall behind him, though, that fear shows much more. His smile drops. I clear my throat in warning when I see Luca getting ready to throw a punch.

Luca glances back at me behind him. When he sees Lyric behind me, he relaxes slightly before glaring fiercely at Joel. "What the fuck are you doing here?"

Joel's eyes flick to me, then back to Luca. "I… I'm getting married, Luca. I met Alicia when she was on a holiday in London. It was fate. We fell in love. Her home is here. So, I guess that means so is mine."

Luca takes a step closer, but I reach out and take his arm. He growls. "You fucking knew this is where we live. I made sure you knew so you'd stay the fuck away from her."

Joel keeps his back against the wall and takes small steps towards the crowded hallway. "Luca, I didn't know she'd be here." His eyes flick to Lyric. My blood runs cold. "Hey, Lyric," he says softly, like he's talking to a deer that might bolt.

She lets out a terrified noise I can only define as a shriek. I feel her fist grip my jacket harder than I ever imagined she could. Her other hand has found its way to the belt of my slacks. She's both gripping and pulling at it as she plasters herself against the wall and me. I ignore the glances she attracts, thankful she doesn't see them. She doesn't need that.

I push her gently behind me a little more and glare viciously at him. "Don't fucking speak to her. Don't look at her. Don't go anywhere near her. Got me?" I know my voice is cold and dripping with venom, but I try to keep it low so as to not attract more stares.

Joel's eyes snap to mine, but he ignores the warning. I doubt he can see Lyric behind me, but he speaks directly to her anyway. "Lyric, I'm sorry for what happened," he says quietly.

She lets out a strangled sob I'm sure is far more high-pitched than she'd like. She shakes her head against my back. She's gone from shivering to trembling uncontrollably in terror. I don't doubt that if she weren't between me and the wall, she'd be on the floor curled in a ball.

"Did you not hear him?" Luca nearly yells. "He said don't fucking speak to her! You got that? Mate?"

"I'm s-sorry… S-so… s-so… s-s-sorry…," Lyric mumbles.

I reach behind me and put my hand on her hip as she continues mumbling. I don't take my eyes off Joel. "Do you honestly think apologizing is going to fix anything? Who the fuck do you think you are? You have no fucking idea what damage you've caused her. Do you?"

He shoots me glare. "I don't know who you are, but it doesn't concern you."

I hold out an arm and push Luca back when he tries to lunge for Joel. "Who I am is none of your concern. But if you think for a second I'm going to stand by and allow you to marry Alicia after everything you've done to Lyric, I promise you, you have another thing coming."

"Look. I'm not that same person. Just forget about all of that. I'll stay away from her. Just -"

"Actually, I'd like to hear more about what happened," Chief King says as he comes around the corner. He crosses his arms over his chest, effectively blocking Joel's exit. His glare might be more dangerous than mine and Luca's combined.

I can't help but smirk just a little as I squeeze Lyric's thigh and press her a little more against the wall. Mostly so she can feel me more and know she's safe. But my eyes remain solely on Joel. "Joel, here, is Lyric's ex. The same ex I made mention of to you."

"You didn't provide much detail, *Captain* Rens." Chief King's lips twitch when Joel gasps at hearing that I'm a Captain. I know he made sure that one word was enunciated perfectly and stood out to that fucker. "Just that you were seeing someone who had a very violent ex. Someone who'd done a lot of physical, emotional, and mental damage to her."

Joel's eyes widen. He looks pleadingly at the Chief. "Mr. King, what happened in the past was long ago! I'd never do anything like that again!"

"Like… what… again?" a soft voice says from behind her father. I look behind Chief King to see Alicia standing there. Behind her, we've managed to attract quite the audience. Alicia looks at us all in confusion.

"Alicia! There you are!" Mrs. King says. "What are you doing out here? I sent your father to search -" She looks at each of us in turn, just as confused as her daughter. "What's happening?"

"Joel was just about to tell us how he and our lovely event planner are acquainted," Chief King says, unmoving and unflinching. I fucking love the guy.

"What is going on here?" another voice I don't recognize says. Lyric bursts into uncontrollable sobs.

"I need you to get everyone into the ballroom, please." Chief King's voice is level. He doesn't look at the woman speaking, but I have a feeling it's Lyric's boss.

"Please," Mrs. King says. "Get everyone into the ballroom."

The woman watches us for a moment before she finally nods and does what she's told. No one says a word until everyone is out of the hallway. The only sound is Lyric sobbing hysterically behind me.

"Joel? What's going on?" Alicia asks quietly.

"Yes, Joel. Please. Explain to us all what's happening," Chief King says.

Joel looks more and more terrified as the moments pass. "Uh…"

"The fuck is going on?" Matt growls when he steps around the corner and sees Lyric.

"Matt," I say dead calmly. "Meet Joel Trent. Lyric's ex."

Matt gives Joel a vicious glare as he carefully steps around Alicia and her mother. "Lyric," he whispers. "Come with me, honey. Okay?"

I step forward enough for Matt to block Joel from her view. He wraps her in his arms and leads her protectively away, thanking all of the Gods that Matt knows what was needed without the command being under. And even more thankful that Lyric trusts him as much as me and went with him without a fight, feeling just as safe. I breathe a quiet sigh of relief that she's no longer near this. No longer near him.

"Joel?" Alicia asks again. Her mom wraps her arms around Alicia's waist.

"Joel Trent, is Lyric's ex," Luca finally spits out. "He used to be my friend. I thought he loved my sister."

"I did, Luca," Joel chokes out. I might feel something like empathy, but I know he's trying to make everyone feel bad for him. Fuck if any of us will. Fuck. I take that back. I wouldn't feel shit for him.

"Really? You loved her so much that when she was unsure of something, you'd slap her upside the head?" Luca yells the words loud enough that Joel jumps. "You loved her so much that you pushed and shoved her away from you when she needed to feel that you loved her. So hard that she'd hit the wall. Or the floor. Or crash through a fucking table!" He starts towards Joel again, but he's no match for me. I grab his arms and keep him away, though, I'd love nothing more than to watch him pummel the fucker. "You loved her so much that as punishment for forgetting things, you'd slap her so hard across the head, she'd pass out. Or you'd fuck her so hard in the ass, she'd bleed! You loved her so much that you thought trying to drown her while raping her was the best way to show it!"

Joel's face has turned white. Alicia is crying into her mother's neck. Chief King looks like he might throw up. Luca's face is red with anger as he fights me to get to Joel. Joel looks like he wants to flee. I don't blame him. I'd want to flee if I were him, too. Especially since I know there's way more going on here. Something he wants to keep secret. It's the only logical explanation for him showing up here ready to get married. I don't know how long they've been together, but I do know he's only been in the United States a few months.

I look at Luca. "Stop," I command. "I know how fucking pissed you are, but you need to trust me."

He glares but backs down. "Fuck," he growls.

I turn to Joel. "There's no way you would fall in love, move to the United States, and get married in what? Three months? Especially not to the Police Chief's daughter."

"Three months?" Alicia looks confused. "We met on Facebook. Over two years ago. I went to London a year ago today to meet him. My mom came with me. We made a vacation of it."

Joel looks panicked. "Alicia is right."

"But you said you met in London. And you haven't been here that long." I narrow my eyes. "You apparently fell madly in love."

Alicia shakes her head. "What is going on? Joel?"

"Explain. Now." Chief King is getting agitated.

Joel glances at Luca before taking a breath. "Son of a bitch." He scrubs his hands down his face.

Luca scoffs. "You met on Facebook two fucking years ago. When you were still with Lyric. I don't know why that doesn't surprise me."

"You were with Lyric? Like the event planner Lyric?" Alicia looks more and more confused as the seconds go by.

Joel takes a deep breath. "Yes. I was. But it was a long time ago, Alicia. Our relationship was on the rocks when you and I started talking. When you came to London to meet me, Lyric and Luca had already moved. Our relationship was long over."

"But you knew she was here!" Luca yells before lunging at him again. I, once again, am forced to hold him back. "You told me you'd stay the fuck away from her! You gave me your goddamn word!"

Joel glares at him. "To keep your ass out of jail for assaulting me!"

"Enough!" Chief King yells. "From the beginning. Now."

I let Luca go once more and turn towards Joel. "You're going to tell him everything you did. Because if you don't, I will. And you'll be in handcuffs when I do it because I have a feeling the reason you're getting married so fucking quickly after showing up here is to avoid some shit that happened in the United Kingdom. What was it, Joel? Did you beat up another girl?"

His sharp intake of breath is all I need to know that I'm on the right track.

And my blood turns instantly to ice.

Chapter Thirteen

✮ Lyric ✮

I gulp in the air. I can't get enough of it. Or maybe it's too much. Maybe I'm taking in too much oxygen and not dispelling enough carbon dioxide!

I cough as my eyes widen in panic.

"Lyric. Look at me." Matt's deep and powerful voice is calm and cuts through my racing thoughts. He puts both hands on my cheeks and forces my eyes to focus on his. "My eyes. What color are they?"

I blink a few times and focus on Matt. "B-brown."

"Good girl. Look at Mariah. Tell me what color her eyes are." He wipes my eyes with the pad of his thumb as I look at Mariah. She smiles softly and runs her thumb over my hand.

"Uh… um…" I take a deep breath and force myself to focus on Mariah. "B-blue. W-with green a little. And a l-little gold."

"Good. Good girl. Now look at me."

I sniffle and look at him. "S-sorry."

"Ssh…" He shakes his head. "None of that. I get you're scared. I don't blame you. He did some very fucked up shit to you. But you want to know something?"

I nod slowly as he pushes my hair out of my face. "Y-yes."

"I know you. And I know that you're a strong as hell woman. Tenacious. I know that everything that happened to you made you into this incredible, beautiful warrior. I know that you can stand up and face that fucker. Because you're tough. And because, this time, you aren't alone. You have me. You have Mariah. You have Luca. And you have DJ." He glances towards the door to the office we're in. "You have damn near the entire Gainesville Police Department behind you." He looks back at me.

I take another breath as my mind begins to clear. "I-I'm strong," I whisper.

"So strong," Mariah says. She kisses my cheek and squeezes my hand.

Matt lets his hands fall to my upper arms. "Say that again."

"I'm s-strong."

He smiles and squeezes my arms lightly. "So fucking strong. Say it again."

I take another breath and begin to feel more and more calm. "I'm strong." I close my eyes and open them again. "I'm strong." I take another breath as my eyes widen. "I can't let Alicia marry him. She'll be in danger! What if he already did something to her?"

Mariah and Matt both smile. Matt kisses my forehead. "There she is," he whispers. "There's that fearless woman you've turned into."

I nod and blush. "I have to tell them. He won't tell them the truth. She'll need to hear it."

"DJ will tell them. And Luca," Mariah says, giving my hand a squeeze.

I shake my head. "No. I have to be the one. She'll want to hear it from me. It will be more effective. And she'll be upset. Maybe... Maybe I can help her through it."

Before I can talk myself out of it, I take another calming breath. I walk with purpose to the door and open it. I don't need to look behind me to know Matt and Mariah are behind me. I trust that they are and always will be at my side.

So, with Matt and Mariah with me, I march my way back to the hallway Joel is trapped in. I am strong. I am brave. I will not allow him to prey on anyone the way he did me. He will never get that opportunity again. I have the control now. I have the power to stop him.

"I-I... No... No! I didn't touch anyone else. I left because I fell in love. End of story! Now, get the fuck away from me. Alicia. Baby, don't listen to them. This should be the happiest day of our lives. Don't let them ruin it." Joel is pleading with Alicia when I walk up behind the crowd of people surrounding Joel.

My heart races, but I know he can't hurt me. Never again. Alicia's parents keep Joel from her by blocking his path. DJ and Luca are on his other side. Joel looks terrified and pissed all at the same time.

"I want answers, boy. I want them now," Chief King says. He still has his arms crossed over his chest. I can tell by his posture that he's seething.

I clear my throat. "Maybe I can help," I say quietly. I can hear the slight tremor in my voice, but I refuse to allow it to stop me.

DJ's eyes immediately meet mine. "Lyric."

I hold my head high and weave my way through the others to DJ. When his arms wrap around me, I feel myself relax. I feel his strength coursing through me like a gentle wave. Warming me almost. Making it so I not only feel safe, but also steady.

I make a point to look at Joel before Alicia. "Joel and I dated for a while back in the United Kingdom. I knew him for a long time before. He was Luca's friend. Like family, really. Joel helped me recover from a crappy relationship. I thought he was incredible. When we started dating, I honestly thought he was the one. He'd stuck by me for so long. Most of my life, but a lot more over the six or seven years after I got out of that relationship. After we started dating, we began talking about moving in together and marriage. Joel meant the world to me. And I felt like I did to him."

Luca makes a low growling noise. "Turned out to be quite the asshole."

"Alicia. Come on. Don't listen to her. She's jealous of us." Joel speaks low and directly to Alicia.

I ignore him and continue talking directly to Alicia. "He started talking down to me, though. Truthfully, it's all I knew anyway. It wasn't any different. He would build me up and make me feel like the most incredible woman in the world. Then he'd break me down. He called me stupid when I didn't do something right. He'd slap me, but to keep Luca from seeing the bruises, he'd do it upside my head. Hard. Sometimes, I'd see stars. I'd get blurry vision. He knocked me out a couple of times."

Alicia makes a strangled noise I can only classify as a sob. "My God." To her credit, she doesn't look away from me.

I force myself to stay brave. Strong. I know my voice is betraying me. I can feel it tremble every time I ignore a sob and choke it down. I know DJ hears it, too, because he keeps squeezing me. Like he wants me to know he's with me.

"Alicia, this is ridiculous. She's lying to you. She doesn't want us to get married. She wants me for herself."

I close my eyes for a moment and let myself breathe in his scent. When I open them again, I focus once more on Alicia, ignoring Joel. "I started to have memory problems. I'd forget things like where my keys were. Once, I forgot an appointment. When I started forgetting things, Joel's punishments got worse. He'd berate me. He'd slap me in the head. He'd push me. But I always took it as a punishment that I deserved for being bad and upsetting him. I honestly didn't know any better. I grew up being bullied and abused. Luca…" I pause to give my brother a small smile before turning back to Alicia. I can see the tears in her eyes. "Luca is my brother. He's the only one who ever treated me the way I should be. He's always protected me and did what he could to make me see my worth. But that only goes so far when every other important person in your life, especially the man you love, treats you like shit. Makes you feel stupid and fat by his actions and words."

The tears she's fought start falling. She turns into her mother and buries herself in her neck. "So awful," she whispers.

I nod slowly and keep my eyes on her. She's the reason I'm doing this. To protect her. To make sure she doesn't face the same treatment and behavior I did. It took me so long to realize that's not love. It's not a relationship. It took DJ, a real man, to make me see it.

"Alicia," Joel starts. His voice breaks. I glance at him and see real tears in his eyes.

I shake my head. I won't allow him to break me. She needs to know what he did. She needs to know it all. Things that only four people in my life know. "He r-raped me. Several times. I d-didn't v-view it as rape. I viewed it as a p-punishment. I blamed myself for all of it. Even w-when he tried to dr-drown me while he was r-raping me." It's then my own tears finally break.

Alicia falls to the floor in a heap as she cries. Her mother sinks with her. I can tell by the rise and fall of her shoulders that she's crying, too. Chief King looks like he's going to throw up. Matt and Mariah are looking at me so proudly. Luca is glaring fiercely at Joel. DJ has his lips against my neck and is swaying gently with me. Joel is shooting daggers at me.

But I don't stop. I won't. I can't. "He had the shower running over my head. And the bathtub full. Luca saved my life. Joel was put in the hospital that night. But he could have k-killed me. He tried to." I pause to compose myself. Alicia is crying hysterically. "I'm sorry. I'm so sorry for how you had to find out," I sniffle. "I felt like I needed to be the one to tell you." After a few moments and a couple of deep breaths, I look the Chief dead in the eyes. "I have PTSD. I have nightmares of his hands around my throat. I still sometimes feel like I'm stupid and deserve to be punished somehow for something that isn't my fault. And that's beyond the needs I already have that's... difficult to explain." I look up at DJ a moment before back at the Chief. "That's the truth of what happened. Luca beat the shit out of him to protect me. Joel knew if he went to the police, I had two witnesses to his abuse and attempted murder. He'd never win in court."

"I made an agreement with him," Luca picks up where I left off. "He stayed away from Lyric. I stayed away from him. It was simple. When we got our Visas to come here, I told him where we planned to settle. I told him if he ever thought to come for a holiday, to stay the fuck away from Gainesville." He levels Joel with another glare that has him looking away from me. "Obviously, he didn't heed the warning."

"That still doesn't answer my question? What happened that made you come here and want to get married so fucking fast?" DJ growls. "Who was the other girl you beat the shit out of?"

Joel's eyes snap to DJ's. "I... didn't -"

"Bullshit." I can feel his deep voice rumbling in his chest. I'm not entirely certain what he knows, but I stay quiet because I trust him. "They say I'm a human bullshit detector. I can sniff out a lie better than a lie detector test. You're lying. There's a fucking reason. You're either going to tell us, or I'll haul your ass in and lock you up while I call my buddies at ICE and -"

"No!" Joel says. I narrow my eyes at the sudden panic. "Not the State Department or ICE. Okay? I'll... I'll tell you. I'll tell you what you want to know." He looks at Chief King as he slides down the wall. He sits on the floor and shakes his head. When he takes a breath, I can see he looks defeated. Weakened.

"I... can't... I can't listen to this anymore." Alicia stands and darts away from us. Her mother follows her. I start to follow her, too. My heart is broken for her. I know how she must feel.

DJ tightens his grip. "Let her mom. When she's ready to talk about it, she'll come to you. I've known Alicia since she was just a kid. She just needs to be alone right now."

"Okay." I melt into him.

"Start talking," Matt growls.

Joel looks up at us all. Except me. He avoids looking at me at all costs. After a few moments he looks at the wall in front of him. "My parents introduced me to this girl. They wanted me to marry her. Something about a good alliance between our families. By that time, I had already avoided jail time and met Alicia. We were planning to meet. But my parents were forcing this girl on me. I thought if I scared her enough, she'd leave. But she didn't. She was like Lyric. She took all-out beatings as punishment. No matter what I did, she came crawling back. It made me sick to my stomach. She. She made me sick to my stomach. How the fuck could anyone think being slapped or kicked was punishment?"

"I think I'm going to be sick," Mariah whispers. She puts a hand over her mouth and grips Matt's arm before she darts to the bathroom across the lobby. I expect Matt to follow, but he doesn't.

Instead, he crosses his arms over his chest. "Then what?" he growls.

"She's okay," DJ whispers when he notices me staring at the bathroom Mariah ran into. "The squeeze of Matt's arm told him to continue. She'll be okay."

I nod, relieved. "Thank you," I whisper.

"The last one went too far. I knocked her out, but I thought she was dead. I ran. I called the cops. I hid at my parent's house. They took her to the hospital and came looking for me. My parents wanted to protect me. So, they hid me. When Alicia came to meet me, my parents decided the best way to protect me was a Fiancé Visa. They helped us apply for it.

They paid all the fees. After it was approved, I needed to be married within ninety days and needed a sponsor. That's why this wedding seems so quick, but we were planning it for a little longer. Alicia makes enough to sponsor me, so she did."

"The fuck she did that without my permission," Chief King growls.

Joel flinches but looks up at him. "Yes, sir. She did. She signed all the papers she needed to. She paid whatever she needed to. My parents wired her the money to reimburse her."

"How the hell did he get a Visa when the police in the UK are looking for him?" Matt asks.

"Simple," DJ answers.

"His parents," Luca finishes.

"They wanted to stay out of the drama. So, to everyone that mattered, including the Government, they'd disowned me. They used a random person on the street to wire the money to Alicia. And paid them handsomely. They also paid off a lot of people. As far as I know, the cops aren't looking for me anymore. And if they are, they don't have a case because the girl won't press charges. My family is too powerful."

"So, you're going to sit here and tell me that you coming here was a coincidence. That it had nothing to do with Lyric." DJ's grip tightens around me.

Joel slowly stands. "Nothing. At all."

Matt chuckles. "They call DJ a human lie detector. They call me a fucking truth hound. You're lying. This had more to do with her than you're letting on."

Joel shakes his head. "No. Nothing." He gets brave and tries to push past Matt, but Matt isn't having any of it.

Matt shoves Joel back so hard that he hits the wall. "Try again," he growls dangerously.

My eyes widen, and I whimper. "Matt. Don't."

"You can't do that to me! I'll have your badge for that!" Joel bellows.

Matt laughs. "You think so, huh?"

Chief King, who hasn't so much as moved an inch, suddenly has his arm against Joel's throat. "Funny thing. His boss is standing right here." He lets up a little when Joel sputters. "Now you're going to be a good boy and turn the fuck around. I'm sure the guys in the United Kingdom will be happy to get you back. No way in all of Hell you're getting a Visa to stay in my country and be anywhere near my daughter or this young lady."

"But -"

Matt grins and cuts a surprised and frightened as fuck Joel off. "Stop talking and answer the question. How does Lyric fit in your little plan?" Matt spins him and has him in cuffs faster than I can blink.

"Get off me!" Joel yells.

Matt slams his head against the wall. "Whoops. Sorry about that."

"Ouch! Bloody fuck!" Joel yells again. "You all saw that!"

"Saw what?" Chief King asks.

"I didn't see a fucking thing," DJ says. I know he's smiling. I can't help but grin myself. Seeing Joel finally in handcuffs where he belongs is everything I ever wanted for him, but didn't know I needed to see.

"Get the fuck off me!" Joel tries to pull away, but he's not as strong as Matt.

Matt easily shoves him into the wall again. "I could do this all day, but maybe I'll let Lyric take a shot. I'm sure she'd enjoy a few kicks to your precious, tiny dick."

I can't stop the giggle that escapes when Matt turns Joel towards me. "I'd love to."

Joel gives me a terrified look that makes my heart literally take flight. I need that. I needed to see his fear. "Okay! I'll tell you! It was two birds with one stone. I got Alicia. Her money. Her status here. Her family power. And I thought I could easily get Luca to hit me. It would get him arrested and his Visa revoked. Lyric would have been completely defenseless. I knew I could intimidate her into shutting the fuck up about everything that happened. Luca would be deported. Lyric would be alone." He tries to glare but drops his head instead. I'm sure it's because DJ's own glare is far more vicious and dangerous.

As I watch Matt and Chief King lead Joel away, I feel vindicated. For the first time in my entire life, I'm finally seeing someone who hurt me get everything they deserve and more. I've never felt happier or lighter. I've never felt more free of my past. Like the chains and shackles that hold me to it are finally broken. Like I can finally move on with my life without the fear of my past coming back to haunt me.

I feel like I'm finally free to love and be loved like I deserve. I look up at DJ and turn to hug him. When he holds me tightly to his body, I feel nothing but something I've only felt in small amounts. I just feared it would be ripped away again. I feel…

Hope.

Epilogue

☆ DJ ☆

(One Year Later)

I moan. My eyes roll back in my head. Sensations only Lyric can make me feel shoot down my spine to the tip of my dick. My stomach tightens. Her tongue does things that have to be fucking outlawed. My head falls back.

"Fuck…" I close my eyes and grip her hair.

"Mmm…" She licks from my balls all the way up my length, nipping and sucking along the vein that runs up my cock until she reaches my tip.

She dips her tongue into the dimple just below my tip as she pumps my cock faster and faster. She takes my tip into her mouth and swirls her tongue around while she sucks. Hard. I see stars and tighten my grip on her hair.

"Lyric. Fuck, baby, I'm gonna come."

She nips my tip and moves her hand down my length. She trails her other hand slowly and seductively down my abs and across my thigh until she reaches my balls. She's taken as much of me into her mouth as she can.

She plays with my balls and starts bobbing her head up and down. When my dick touches the back of her throat, she swallows. She's pumping the part of my dick she can't get into her mouth at the same pace she's bobbing her head.

"Mmm…," she moans, sending the vibration from her throat down my shaft and into my balls.

"Oh, fuck." I look down at her and push her head into me as I start to come. That tingling in my spine turns to a lightning bolt. I spurt into her mouth and watch her as she swallows every drop, sucking me dry.

When she's done, she looks up at me through her sexy lashes. She flicks her tongue across her lips. "Mmm… Yummy."

I grin. "What happened to the whole unlucky to see the bride on her wedding day thing?"

Lyric laughs as she crawls up my body. "It's only unlucky if you see her in her wedding dress before you're meant to."

I wrap my arms around her. "Aww… I see now. So, the bride can give and be given as many orgasms as she desires, so long as the groom doesn't see her in her wedding dress before she walks down that aisle."

She giggles. "See? Now you're getting it." She smiles and leans down to kiss me as she wraps her arms around me.

I pull her down on top of me and hug her close to me. I know she loves cuddling and snuggling after anything sexual. It's how she knows she did a good job. She thrives on knowing she pleases me. Anyone, really. She loves doing things for others and making them happy.

I'd do anything for her on any given day, but today is extra special. Today is the day she walks down that aisle and becomes my wife. Mine in every sense of the word. For all of eternity. I've never been excited to marry anyone, but fuck. I can't wait to marry her. I've waited my whole life for her.

I run my hands up and down her back and kiss her head when she settles. I'm so fucking proud of her. We've been together now for just over a year. In that time, Lyric has turned into damn near an entirely different woman. She slips sometimes, but it's nothing a spanking doesn't fix. Lyric responds very well to them.

I don't have a fucking clue why I thought to spank her the first time I did it. I've never done that before with anyone. But nothing I've done with her has been close to things I'm used to. Everything with her is brand new. The spanking just felt like something I was supposed to. I didn't realize at the time that it centers her when she feels like she's spiraling out of control. It's like it brings her back to herself. I suspected it, though.

She's become so fucking strong since her showdown with Joel. Joel was deported back to the United Kingdom where he faced charges for his actions against the girl his parents wanted him to marry. Apparently, no amount of money can shut-up a pissed off mother. No matter how much that mother's husband begs. The girl's mother wouldn't let her husband sweep anything under the rug. The police had never stopped looking for Joel. But Joel's father did pay off enough people in the State Department to get him that Visa.

It's too bad for him that it got revoked. It's also too bad that the family of the girl he beat up has just as much money as his. The only reason they'd stayed quiet for the amount of time they did is because the girl's father was trying to continue with the merger, or whatever the hell they were trying to do. When there was no chance of it going forward, mostly because of the outcry of the girl's mother, her father backed off and threw everything he had at securing an attorney to take Joel down.

When he was deported, the police were waiting for him when he stepped off the plane in the United Kingdom. That may have been because he was escorted there by Chief King himself. He was promptly arrested and admitted to what he did.

Lyric gave a statement when the police reached out to her. It was only because he also admitted to what he did to her. I'm pretty sure he admitted to everything because he felt beaten down and intimidated. But it wouldn't have mattered because ICE, the United States Immigration and Customs Enforcement, took statements from all of us regarding the day of the wedding.

It seemed like Lyric dropped a ton of baggage she had been carrying. As soon as she got through her interview with them and gave her statement to them and the police in the United Kingdom, she very obviously started breathing easier. When we found out he was convicted of assault of the other girl and the attempted murder of Lyric herself, she cried in relief for three days straight.

Luca studies every day for his citizenship test. He still does construction things, but he volunteers his time instead. He decided he wanted to really pursue his cooking passion. So, he's now the in-house caterer for the Historical Thomas Center. It's a good job. He's doing what he wants and is there for Lyric if she needs someone.

She's become incredibly close to Mariah and Alicia. The three of them do a lot of things together. They've both helped Lyric in opening up and learning to trust. She's never had real friends. She's also become incredibly close to Matt. I couldn't be happier about her inner circle if I wanted to be.

Lyric shifts and straddles me. She sits up and traces my abs as she watches me. I put my hands behind my head and smile up at her. She's beyond beautiful. She's gotten back to a far healthier weight. I can tell she's much happier and feels better about herself. She picks herself apart a lot less. There are still things she doesn't like about herself, but instead of obsessing about it and saying she's ugly or something, she comes to me and asks how to fix it.

She currently doesn't like how she feels weak if she's not able to lift something without her arms getting tired. So, we're working on strengthening and conditioning her arms and gaining a little muscle.

"What are you thinking about, beautiful?" I ask.

She smiles softly. "How I'm going to look in my dress." She frowns a little and looks at her arms. They aren't quite where she wants them to be. She thinks they're too skinny.

"I thought Mariah solved that problem. Something about sleeves."

She shrugs slowly. "Kind of. You can still see them. I don't want anyone to make fun of them and call them small."

I can't help but chuckle as I slowly sit up. I put my arms around her and kiss her. Softly at first, then deeply, tangling her tongue with mine and sucking lightly. She moans quietly and lets her hands trail up my abs to my chest before she locks them around my shoulders and submits completely to my kiss.

I pull back only when we're both breathless. I reach up and tuck a lock of hair behind her ears. "You are beautiful."

She blushes and ducks her head. "I know…," she whispers without meeting my eyes.

I tangle my fingers in her hair and tug lightly until she's looking at me. "Tell me. Say the words."

She lowers her eyes but looks up at me through her lashes. "I am beautiful," she says quietly.

I smile and kiss her softly. "Tell me again."

"I am beautiful," she says a little more confidently.

I kiss her again, a little more deeply. I nip her lip as I pull away. "Tell me again. I'm not sure I believe that you believe the words."

She blushes a little deeper shade of red, but looks me directly in the eyes. "I am beautiful." She nods decisively and smiles with confidence.

I grin. "There's my beautiful girl." I lean in and kiss her deeply and passionately. She presses against me and down, making my dick hard for her almost instantly. But just when I'm about to slide into her, someone knocks on my door.

She whimpers when she sees the time. "That would be Matt and Mariah."

I growl low at the second knock, debating if we have time for a quickie as my dick twitches and begs to be inside her. "We should probably let them in."

She giggles when I don't take my own advice and kiss her instead. When she pulls away, she's smiling. "We're getting married."

I grin again and run my fingers through her hair. "Yes. We are."

"Mariah really wants to pamper me."

"I can think of other ways to pamper you."

She giggles when the knocking becomes more insistent. I can imagine Matt standing there incessantly knocking while he grins like an idiot and Mariah laughs. They know what we're up to, I'm sure.

Lyric gives me a quick kiss before getting up. She grabs something and wraps it around herself as I sigh. After a couple of moments, I get up and grab a pair of boxer briefs. I start to follow, but decide against it. I really don't want Matt or Mariah to see the hard on I'm sporting. I grab a pair of loose sweats and throw them on.

When I head downstairs, Mariah and Lyric both run up them and pass me, giggling. I shake my head and smile. I don't want to know what

Mariah has planned. I'm sure it's a bunch of girly things, but as long as Lyric is happy, I'm happy.

"Couldn't be bothered with a shirt?" Matt teases.

"Fuck you," I growl. I'm trying to be grouchy, but Matt knows me too well. He knows I'm anything but.

He laughs. "Pissy we interrupted morning sex?"

I grin and laugh. "We were just getting there. Contemplated leaving your asses outside while we finished."

"Don't blame you. I'd have done the same thing."

We both laugh as I start making a strawberry banana shake. "Where's Mariah taking her?" I ask while I throw chopped up fruit into the blender.

"Massages, then hair."

"No breakfast?"

"Nope. Mariah said neither of them intend to eat much until the reception. She has a fruit tray for when they get to the Historical Thomas Center to get dressed and have their hair done." He glances at the blender when I start blending. When I'm done, he chuckles. "You ain't letting her out of the house without something."

I chuckle because that was absolutely not a question. Matt is just as strict with nutrition as I am. "No. I had a feeling that's what you were going to say." I grab a to-go tumbler and pour the shake into it. I put a straw into the hole it belongs in and glance up when Mariah and Lyric race excitedly down the stairs.

Matt laughs. "I did the same thing to Mariah this morning. Hers is in her car."

I watch as Lyric and Mariah laugh together. She starts putting on her shoes as Mariah chatters. After a second, Lyric races over to me. She gives me a quick kiss and hug. Mariah does the same with Matt.

"Love you! See you soon, handsome!" Lyric turns and excitedly walks towards the door when Mariah grabs her hand.

"Stop," I command, dominantly. Both Mariah and Lyric stop in their tracks and look back at me with wide eyes. I look directly at Lyric. "What are you forgetting?"

She blinks adorably at me as she thinks. "Um…"

I point to the shake. "You know my rule."

Her eyes widen in realization as she nods and reaches for the shake. "Sorry. I was really excited."

I smile and step forward to kiss her. "I know." I nip her lip. "Now go enjoy your pampering. I'll see you at the altar."

She giggles and smiles brightly as she takes a drink of her shake and follows Mariah outside. I smile after her. My heart is so full of love for her, it feels like it might burst. When she closes the door, I start making my own shake.

"Alright, groom. What's our plan for the day?" Matt asks.

I grin. "I ain't the best man. That's all on you."

Matt laughs. "Well, I planned on taking you to breakfast, but it looks like you have that covered."

I laugh. "I can freeze this." I finish making it and turn to put my tumbler in the freezer.

"Grab your tux. We'll have to take your car because Mariah wanted to drive and wanted her car. We can drop your car at my house and swap it out for my truck if you want me to drive."

"Yeah. Whatever you want to do. I'm at your mercy."

Matt cracks up as I jog upstairs. "Dangerous fucking words!"

✫✫✫

Standing at the altar waiting for my beautiful bride gives me a few moments to check out everything. Lyric worked very hard to make everything perfect for both of us. The altar I'm standing under is lush and green. It smells a lot like fern. Purple lilies, bluebells, and white baby's breath are twined throughout the green of the fern.

Behind us is a marble fountain giving off a very soft and soothing sound. Purple wildflowers are intertwined with the shrubbery. In front of me is the center that connects the two buildings of the Historical Thomas Center. There's a path for Lyric to walk down that's covered in lavender lily petals and bluebells, which Mariah is being so kind as to drop on her way down the aisle.

I glance at Matt. He's grinning like an idiot as he watches Mariah. I can't help but smile because she hasn't taken her eyes off him either.

Their love is something beyond epic. I can only hope to reach their level with Lyric.

Mariah's dress is lavender, long, flowing, and strapless. It hugs every single one of her curves. I can't tell if it's silk or satin, but it moves so well with her that I don't think Matt's eyes are the only ones captivated by her. Her bouquet is a mix of purple lilies, bluebells, and baby's breath.

Matt's tux matches mine. We're both wearing black slacks with white, button-down, long-sleeve shirts. We have matching lavender vests that pair perfectly with the color of Mariah's dress. The only thing that separates our outfits is the purple lily I have tucked into the left breast-pocket of my vest.

When the melody of "Husavik" by Molly Sanden starts, everyone stands in anticipation of the bride. When Lyric turns the corner and Luca starts leading her down the few stairs, my breath catches. I'm pretty sure everyone else is, too.

"Holy... shit," Matt whispers.

"My... God...," I whisper.

Lyric's dress is pure white with a sweetheart neckline. It hugs her upper body and flows from her waist to her ankles. It's light and billows in the light breeze. True to her word, Mariah took care of the sleeves. The dress has delicate straps. Attached to the straps are sleeves that are made of some soft, see-through fabric. Lace maybe? Her hair is down, but whoever did her hair has managed to lace lilies, bluebells, and baby's breath throughout it to match the bouquet she's carrying. I figured she'd be wearing something sparkly, but not my girl. She's very simple and even manages to make the simple flowers look stunning.

When she reaches me, she smiles shyly and looks up at me through her lashes. She's not wearing a veil, so there is no barrier between me and her beautiful face. I grin down at her and push a stray tendril of hair behind her ear. I'm vaguely aware of Luca putting her hand in mine and saying something. I'm completely lost in Lyric.

"You're beautiful," I whisper, my voice cracking.

Her eyes glitter with unshed tears of happiness. "So are you," she whispers, effectively making my heart soar.

I barely hear anything the officiant says. It's not until Matt hands me Lyric's ring that my reverie is broken. I take her small, perfect, soft as silk hand in mine and slip the band on her finger. It's white-gold. There are thirteen small blue sapphires. It matches her engagement ring. A diamond sits in the middle of a white-gold band. On each side are two lines of twelve clear-cut accent diamonds. In the middle of the two lines of accent diamonds are five slightly larger sapphires.

I'll never forget the second I gave it to her. Her eyes lit up. Her hands trembled, much like they are now. She smiled so brightly, she could have easily given light to the darkness of our vast universe.

"Lyric. The second I saw you, I knew I was in trouble. Big trouble. I knew if I ever saw you in person, it would be the end for me. I avoided it at all costs. But fate had other plans. And it didn't give a shit about what I wanted. It obviously knew what I needed better than I did. I needed you. I didn't know it. At least my head didn't." I reach up and cup her cheek with one hand while the other holds her hand. I gently caress the back of her hand. She leans into the one cupping her cheek. "I fell so far in love with you, it knocked the wind out of me. I tried to deny it, but the truth was I couldn't wait to get to know you. And since that day, I've fallen more and more in love with you. I love you more today than I did yesterday. I'll love you more tomorrow than I do today. I can't wait to spend the rest of my life with you. Always and forever."

I wipe Lyric's tears away with the pad of my thumb as she takes my ring and slips it on my finger. It's a titanium band with a blue ion accent channel spanning the entire circumference of the middle of the ring.

She holds my hand in one of hers and reaches up to wipe away my tears with the pad of her thumb. "DJ. I think I was in love with you before I ever actually met you. I had never seen you in a picture or life, but I'd heard so much about you. When I met you, that was it for me. I didn't know for sure who you were, but I figured it out when I saw you with Luca. You've been with me through all of my storms. No matter how rough it got, you never left me. You steadied me. You became my rock. You became my home. I never felt alone or worthless. You've always made me feel like the most important person in the world to you. Even when things were busy, or you got involved in a huge case or something. You always made sure that I came first. No one but Luca has ever done that for me. It scared me at first, but it quickly became my normal. It became my…" she pauses as she thinks of the words. "It became my perfect. You. You became my perfect. I feel like I've always loved you.

Like our souls are connected. I'll love you for the rest of my life, DJ. Always and forever."

I smile and barely resist the need to lean down and kiss her with every ounce of love that I feel for her. I hold back as the officiant finishes our ceremony, but when he finally gives me permission to kiss my bride, I waste no time. I lean down and kiss her. My arm wraps around her waist. My other hand grips the back of her neck. My tongue slips between her satin lips and tangles with hers.

Very suddenly, I'm filled with a desire that isn't going to be satisfied with a kiss. I need every part of her. I need to feel her in my arms. I need her nails digging into my shoulders and across my back. I need her. Just her. My wife. Mine.

While our friends and family stand, whistling and applauding, I bend and lift Lyric in my arms. She squeals and laughs as I carry her up the aisle. One thing is on my mind. Not pictures. Not food. Not dancing.

It's her.

Only her.

"Where are you taking me?" Lyric asks. She giggles when I start jogging up the few stairs leading to the room I got dressed in earlier.

"Somewhere I can have you alone." I kick open the door as I kiss her. Hard. I kick the door closed behind me and nip her tongue.

"Mmm...," she moans. She tangles her fingers in my hair and sucks on my tongue.

I gently set her on her feet. I don't stop kissing her. Tasting her. Sweet and spicy. That's my girl. I kiss, lick, and nip my way down her jaw to her neck while I'm undoing my belt. I tug my button open and jam my zipper down, carefully pressing my hard cock against myself so I don't hurt it. Lyric's mouth is all over my neck and throat. Her nails gently scrape along the back of my neck. We're both panting.

I start to unzip her dress, but realize there's no zipper. It's all buttons. I almost whimper, but hold onto what little control I have left long enough to pull up her dress. I bunch it around her waist and lift her.

"I need you," I growl against her neck.

She wraps her legs around my waist. "I always need you," she whispers in my ear. She grips my shoulders and holds tight when I slam my dick into her. "Oh, God, yes..."

I thrust hard, deep, and fast. Every ounce of control I had is gone as soon as her warm and wet walls start pulsing around my cock. Any shred of dignity I had about jumping her in a public place flies out the window.

"Fuck, yes."

She meets every thrust, clenching around me each time I sink into her. She knows how to drive me out of my mind. I slam into her over and over again. I slap her ass then grip it hard. I kiss across her throat to the other side of her neck.

"DJ…" She lets her neck fall to the side, giving me more access to her sensitive skin.

I lick then nip. I kiss up to just below her ear. My fingers dig into her ass. "All mine. Say it."

"Yours. All yours." She bites my shoulder with a soft whimper as she tightens around me. Her pussy clamps around my dick. Her thighs tremble uncontrollably.

I grunt and moan as my eyes roll back in my head. I shift, pinning her against the wall and sliding a hand between us. I start rubbing her clit as I thrust. She screams into my shoulder and bunches my vest into her fist while she bites down.

I don't need to ask her if she's ready. I can feel it by how hard she's clamped around me. With one more hard thrust, I'm buried in her pussy. My whole body is shaking just like hers is. I give her clit a little more pressure as I rub. She jerks into me.

"Come for me, sexy girl."

"DJ!" She screams into my shoulder as she falls over the edge. Her pussy pulses and spasms as her pleasure overtakes her. My dick is instantly soaked.

I wait until I feel her starting to come before I let myself release. "Fuck, Lyric," I moan against her neck. My hips jerk into her with each spasm as I fill her pussy.

She moans and whimpers so sexily as she takes it all that I can't help the last jerk of my dick that fills her pussy a second time. I feel like she's milking everything from me. Like she can't get enough. I know the feeling. A lifetime will never be enough.

After a few moments, I slowly pull out of her. I gently let her down but keep my arms securely around her. She giggles as she adjusts her panties. I grin because I can't help it. She's so beautiful.

"I have no control when it comes to you," she says with another giggle.

I laugh. "Good."

She looks up at me adoringly as we adjust our clothing. I don't know what I did to deserve her, but as I lead her out to our reception, I make another vow. This one to myself.

I'll live my entire life proving to her that I'm worth her trust and her love.

Ever since Lyric crashed into me, I've felt like I've been in some kind of a paradise.

Our paradise.

A place where no one can touch us. Hurt us.

A place just for us.

The End

Next In The Beautiful Dream Series

The sweet and sinfully sexy Beautiful Dream Series continues with *Tactical Inferno*.

Sometimes, I want to run away to a place no one knows me. Where no one will judge me. Somewhere I'll be left alone. Maybe then I could live my life the way I want to.

Even I know that's wishful thinking. My agent would hunt me down. I am contracted for another book, after all. Something to give Alexander's Publishing House, the largest publishers in the world, another bestseller to tuck under their belt.

But when my best friend is murdered in cold blood, writing is the last thing on my mind. The only thing keeping me standing is the woman investigating my friend's murder. Officer Lyric Sharpe.

She's stunning. I can't stop thinking about her.

Before I know it, I become the sole focus of my friend's murderer's attention. And never in a million years would I have guessed who it is.

I have to rely on Lyric and her unmatched instincts and skills in order for me to survive and show her that her love is the greatest gift of all.

Order *Tactical Inferno* Today!

The Beautiful Dream Series

Available Now

Loving You
My Love, My Heart
Softening Lyric
Undercover Temptations
Captain Charming
Breaking Boundaries
Crashing Into You
Tactical Inferno
Ravishing Our Queen
Cherished By The Texan
Unveiling Our Passions

Box Sets Available

The Beautiful Dream Series: Box Set: Part 1
The Beautiful Dream Series: Box Set: Part 2

Other Books By Melony Ann
The Crane Family Series

Available Now

The Reluctant Mafia King
Sweet Lies
Billion Dollar Love Story
Be Mine
Protecting Her
Dangerously Forbidden Love
His Heart
Love In The Dark

Box Sets Available

The Crane Family Series

The Deimos Trilogy

Available Now

Connor's Legacy
Aryan's Alpha
Kade's Redemption

Box Sets Available

The Deimos Trilogy

The Forbidden Temptation Series

Available Now

The Detective's Forbidden Temptation
The Running Back's Forbidden Temptation

The Lucinio Family Series

Available Now

Rising From The Ashes
The Player's Rebel
Encrypting My Heart
Fighting My Fate

Multi Author Series
Piper Falls: Firehouse 49

Available Now

Ignite My Fire by Melony Ann
Regain My Fire by Kindra White
Playing With My Fire by D.L. Howe
Fight My Fire by Darley Collins
Against My Fire by Anneke Boshoff
Relight My Fire by Louise Murchie
Harness My Fire by Ayana Lisbet
Quench My Fire by Havana Wilder

Let's Be Friends

Follow me on

Bookbub

Facebook

Goodreads

Instagram

Tik Tok

Visit my website
www.melonyannauthor.com

Subscribe to my newsletter and get a FREE never-seen-before NOVELLA
just for subscribers!
https://www.melonyannauthor.com/exclusive-content

Join my Facebook Reader Group!
Melony Ann's Sizzling Book Nook
https://www.facebook.com/groups/melonyannssizzlingbooknook

The official Beautiful Dream Series Playlist on YouTube
https://youtube.com/playlist?list=PLGEiD5wbQmDe1z4_FeeKbMLcBkOz
1M4L4

Dedication

Fear is only in our minds. But you never let it take us over. As we hold your hands walking through this life, we know we'll stumble, but you'll never let us fall.

Acknowledgements

Brad - You've always been my strength when I had none. And still, to this day, you manage to find a way to be my strength when I have none. I love you more each and every day.

Laura - I wouldn't be who I am or where I am without you. I hope you know my love for you is limitless and without end.

Jay - You're like a dark angel who constantly swoops in and makes the world stop coming at me. I don't know where Laura and I would be today without you and Brad guiding us and loving us. I love you beyond what I could ever fathom.

Anneke - You gave me the best news the other day. And I have to say, I'm so very proud of you. You're honestly so strong and brave. I'm honored to call you family.

Jason - You know how superheroes are made up and fiction? Well, I disagree because you're my real life superhero.

Kayla - I don't know how you do what you do, but I'm honestly just impressed by you every single day.

To the Bookstagram Community.

To my family.

To all of those who believe in me and support me.

To all of those who don't.

Cover by: Carter Cover Designs

Edited by: Alyssa Skaggs

About Melony Ann

Melony Ann began writing short stories and poetry as a child. She continued honing her craft over the years until she took the plunge and began publishing her work, despite having severe anxiety.

Melony writes contemporary romance stories that are full of suspense and a lot of steam.

When she isn't writing, she is loving her family and working to make her life something she deserves.

Melony believes that if her writing can inspire just one person, then all of her hard work is worth it.

Her hope is that her writing allows each and every one of her readers to escape for a little while. To dive into a different world one book at a time.